I REMEMBER FALLUJAH

I
REMEMBER
FALLUJAH

FEURAT ALANI

Translated from the French
by Adriana Hunter

OTHER PRESS · NEW YORK

Originally published in French as *Je me souviens de Falloujah* in 2023 by éditions
Jean-Claude Lattès, Paris
Copyright © 2023 Feurat Alani
Translation copyright © 2024 Other Press

Production editor: Yvonne E. Cárdenas
Text designer: Patrice Sheridan
This book was set in Minion Pro and Optima by
Alpha Design & Composition of Pittsfield, NH

1 3 5 7 9 10 8 6 4 2

Library of Congress Cataloging-in-Publication Data
Names: Alani, Feurat, 1980- author. | Hunter, Adriana, translator.
Title: I remember Fallujah : a novel / Feurat Alani ; translated from the French
by Adriana Hunter.
Other titles: Je me souviens de Falloujah. English
Description: New York : Other Press, 2024.
Identifiers: LCCN 2024002626 (print) | LCCN 2024002627 (ebook) |
ISBN 9781635424645 (paperback) | ISBN 9781635424652 (ebook)
Subjects: LCGFT: Novels.
Classification: LCC PQ2701.L27 J4713 2023 (print) | LCC PQ2701.L27 (ebook) |
DDC 843/.92—dc23/eng/20240119
LC record available at https://lccn.loc.gov/2024002626
LC ebook record available at https://lccn.loc.gov/2024002627

For my father, up above.

For my mother and my sister.

For my son who will find his voice someday.

Forgetting is the true winding sheet of the dead.

—GEORGE SAND

Novels are lies that always tell the truth.

—JEAN COCTEAU

PROLOGUE

(October 6, 2019)

MY FATHER had an unvoiced dream: to build a successful life far away from Iraq. That dream fell apart in the 1970s in the subprefecture of Paris.

If you won't collaborate, don't dream, sir.

The dream hung on a small rectangular piece of plastic. A political refugee card brandished by one of the agents. It was a brief exchange.

"It's simple, this card is here, it exists, it belongs to you. But it has a price. We want to know everything about your friends, who they see, their political leanings…"

"In my country, I never betrayed my convictions even though I would have been given a fine career if I had. I won't start doing it here," he replied before putting his beret back onto his head, as if setting his dignity straight right where it belonged, and then he left with a slam of the door.

I wasn't yet born. My father was looking for an adoptive country with no prisons for idealists. He'd ended up in France, imprisoned by a principle he would never contravene: to not betray himself. He wanted asylum, a life far from his own country, an escape from the madmen who governed Iraq; and he had become a political refugee with no status, an exile with no identity card, an immigrant with no future. His broken dreams had wedged themselves deep inside his heart. And the things he had not achieved became things he would not discuss.

The vagaries of life have brought me to write about those things.

FORGETTING

(August 2, 2019)

I'VE NEVER forgotten the day my father lost his memory. I clearly remember the date, which imprinted itself on my life in rainy-day numerals, the date since when nothing has been the same.

Friday, August 2, 2019, in Paris, in room 219 at the Bizet Clinic: It all started with a misunderstanding.

"Aren't you going to wish me a happy birthday?" my father challenged me.

It wasn't his birthday.

"My last year before I hit thirty…" he added.

He wasn't in his twenties.

"I know, I'm talking like an old man trying to escape decrepitude," he concluded.

His voice was cheerful that day. But I didn't recognize the smile hovering on his lips.

He relit his cigarette, tilted up his chin, and offered the packet to me.

"You want a smoke, buddy?"

I'd never touched a cigarette.

"I'm your son, Dad. And I don't smoke, you *know* that."

"Well, what do I know?"

My head suddenly swam.

In his strange rejoinders there was a note of sincerity, a suggestion of accuracy, a hint of truth.

"You sure you don't want a smoke, buddy?" he persisted.

Buddy. I forced a smile. He'd never called me that. I didn't understand right away. Or rather, I didn't want to.

I've never been a smoker, or his buddy. Until that day, I was his son; the only reason he was in room 219 was to have treatment for stage IV lung cancer; and he remembered me. Until that day, my father wasn't an amnesiac.

———

The head of department saw me in a gloomy office. I stepped into it as if into a church, fearful in the face of the Lord. There was no confessional between us, just the unkempt wasteland of a desk. From the full height of his Hippocratic oath, scrawling busily on a notepad, he didn't look up. I stayed standing, watching him. We were both in our graying forties. He wore a white coat by way of a cassock, and I the previous day's shirt crumpled by my overnight anxiety. The lowered blinds were conducive to confidences. I murmured what I had to say as if confessing a sin.

"My father, Rami Ahmed, is losing his memory."

He looked up at last.

"Oh...Mr. Ahmed, room 219?"

"Yes."

"Does he not recognize you?"

"Well, he talks to me like I'm somebody else. Maybe it's only temporary?"

Silence.

I've never liked it when doctors say nothing, or avoid eye contact. It implies anything but agreement.

"If he's really losing his memory, is there a chance he'll recover it?" I reformulated.

He gave the beginnings of a smile.

"There are no chances in science, you know. It's not that straightforward. Unfortunately, there isn't an exhaustive list of disorders of memory. The pathology of each individual amnesiac is different. Some don't remember their childhood. Others lose the more recent past. Sometimes, their memory functions but it's full of holes, like Gruyère cheese. And then things get jumbled—names, places."

"How will we know?"

"You must talk to him. That way you can find out what he's forgotten."

"Do you think this will go on for long?"

"These memory lapses can last from a few minutes to several years. It depends on the type of amnesia—anterograde, retrograde, dissociative, or partial. I'll examine your father, but I'd advise you not to overburden him with too many faces. You have to go about it gradually. If need be, you could make an appointment with our neurologist, he's a hotshot on memory."

If need be. The doctor used the words like someone who rubs elbows with death every day. My father's situation was routine to him, amnesia nothing more than conjecture, a diagnosis, a detail. When someone dear to you is affected by it, you want the world to stop turning. This doctor was in his own world, though, and I didn't have access to it. His telephone rang. He dived back into his work, he seemed very busy. I was no longer in the room. Or I shouldn't have been. Far from having been absolved, I left that office with an additional weight on my shoulders. My head was still ringing with the implacable terms the doctor had used. Before going back to see my father, I typed them into my cell phone. Search engines know no empathy or restraint.

Retrograde amnesia: loss of preexisting memories.

Anterograde amnesia: loss of new memories.

Dissociative amnesia: memory loss caused by trauma or stress.

I didn't know where in all this my strange conversation with my father belonged. I stopped right there. He'd lost his memory, and that was the only thing I knew for sure.

———

Back in room 219, he still looked at me with a stranger's eyes. I tried to explain why, from now on, he would be spending twenty-four hours a day in this clinic. He often used analogies himself so he would understand that he was now a book with many pages torn out, that his memory seemed to have partly disappeared, like a jigsaw puzzle with lots of pieces spirited away by this illness. Then I told him he could ask me as many questions as he liked.

As a child, I was the one who asked him questions: *Who are we? Do I belong in France? Why live if we end up dying? What makes a person a person?* My father took my interrogations seriously, tackled them with concern. To achieve this, he used allegories—particularly when he was drunk—and one of these made a profound impression on me.

One evening he suggested I sit down beside him and he—a man who was a usually nostalgic, often silent drunk—was suddenly garrulous. He'd slipped his headphones down onto his shoulders, and the crackle of an Iraqi *maqam* brightened the living room with its age-old melody. He had decided to shed some light on my questions, as if he'd been pondering them for a while.

His reply—which seemed to me to come straight out of the Hans Christian Andersen fairy tales that I devoured at the time—boiled down to these few sentences: "My son, you and I are travelers. Every traveler carries a suitcase. You can't see the suitcase. It's invisible, but it's there. Over the course of your life, your suitcase will fill up with people, things, memories, and experiences—good ones and bad ones. So that it doesn't get too heavy and you can keep going, you'll have to take out things that are no use to you and keep the most important. You'll have to sort through the suitcase because, with all that weight of words, people, adversity, love, and hate, with the victories and defeats, a traveler's shoulders start to stoop. Identity is a long journey, mine son. It's up to you to make it as light and uncomplicated as possible. But know this, it's not that we *are*. We *become*."

We become. Two words whose power I didn't suspect at the time—how could they summarize existence? *We become* wasn't exactly an answer, it was a tool that I had to use. I've held on to those two words my whole life as if to a climbing rope.

That recollection has dredged another statement from my memory, an impenetrable pronouncement that my father intoned several times, like a series of beacons intended for the traveler I would grow into: *I live with a secret that I will take to my grave.* The before version of my father always made sure I understood what he meant, with the same intensity in his eyes, the same sincerity in his voice, and the same refusal to reveal the secret. So why mention it only to say no more? For a long time, I thought he was toying with me. In room 219, I pondered the question again: Had this secret ever really existed?

I felt an urgent need to get my father—this once taciturn man who was deaf in one ear—to talk, a need to restore his sight, understand him, listen as he related his early life and, who knows, discover this secret taboo that may have been stolen by amnesia. A shameful urge too to satisfy my curiosity. I'd never had access to my father's big narrative. I didn't know about his past. There was no continuity from his story to mine, and the world I'm originally from is completely foreign to me. In our adult conversations, he brushed aside my questions with a sweep of his hand. Instead of the analogies of my childhood, this melancholy man would now reply, "It's too complicated."

On the evening of August 2, 2019, I made him a promise. I would make things easier. We would reclaim the lost memories together.

"Do you remember who you are?" I asked him.

"I'm Rami Ahmed. I was born in Fallujah on January 25, 1944. I left Iraq in 1972."

All sorts of contradictory thoughts came into my mind. What had he forgotten? Had he emptied that invisible suitcase? Would it always be this difficult for him? Should I be unearthing these old stories he never wanted to tell me? There, in that hospital ward, illness had changed all the parameters. Everything had become urgent and necessary. All that was left now were the essentials. A man's story. A son's hopes. Communicating. Memory. And so I started at the beginning that evening. I bought him a notebook. On the first page I wrote some names, as he had for me long ago. *First name: Euphrates. Role* (it occurred to me to put *job*): *son*.

"Dad, I'm your son, my name's Euphrates. You have a wife and a daughter. You have a family. Your wife is Wafa and your daughter, Arwa."

He nodded. "Euphrates...I know the Euphrates."

Snatches of memory may have come back to him, but his meandering amnesia wouldn't allow him to go further. If he was to remember his life, he had to talk to me. I needed to launch him on a subject.

"What's your earliest memory, Dad?" I asked, despite the confusion in his eyes.

This mishap of life gave me hope that I might get to know the man who had kept a veil over his past all through my childhood. Now that the end was drawing near for him, would he finally unpack his invisible suitcase? I waited for his first words. Were we about to speak at last? Reopen the door to Stop Cluny? It turns out that amnesia could be our attenuating circumstance. An unhoped-for opportunity to make up for lost time, to tell each other everything before he went.

My father seemed to remember something, he stammered, thinking out loud. Slowly, as if conjuring his childhood, as if ghosts from the past were appearing before his eyes, as if a dull and distant pain was stirring inside him, he turned and looked me right in the eye. And then at last, fragments of memory pieced together Rami's story.

"I remember Fallujah."

MUHJA

(Summer 1952)

DEATH CAME into Rami's life when he was eight years old, in the form of shrill wailing, women's wails piercing the gloom of Fallujah's dawn. Rami woke with a start. He thought he was hearing the howls of wolves coming after him in his nightmare. Shudders ran up and down his body and the air felt denser; time stood still. Through the bedroom doorway he saw three women dressed entirely in black. She-wolves? Spirits? The howling voices—layered over each other, as terrifying as they were beautiful—cut through his heart again. Blocking his ears made no difference, the pain still bored into his soul. Rami didn't want to go on hearing those voices. An irrepressible urge to escape them propelled him out of his bedroom. He went through the doorway, slipped around the three women, and ran barefoot to the left bank of the Euphrates to be alone. It must have been a *kabous*, a nightmare. But he refused to believe it and couldn't work out whether he should close his eyes or keep them open. So he lay down in the hope of escaping it.

A few minutes later, other more cheerful cries broke the silence in which Rami had taken refuge. Lining up at the end of Fallujah's green bridge, an endless succession of bare-chested boys took turns making acrobatic dives into the Euphrates, which reflected the clear sky. The more fearless of them jumped with a watermelon in their arms to bury it in the silt on the riverbed. This was a local custom in summer, and this year the implacable heat had arrived earlier than expected. The school year was coming to an end, so the diving started first thing in the morning. By nightfall the watermelons would be chilled and ready to be eaten. Rami was struck by how brave and graceful the boys were and thought they couldn't have been much older than twelve.

With all the authority that his eight years allowed him, he sat on the muddy bank next to a small crowd of enthusiastic onlookers to be sure he missed none of the show. Even though he couldn't swim, Rami felt peculiarly drawn to the river that day.

A familiar voice broke through his thoughts. It was coming from the bridge.

"Hey! Over here! Look!"

Rami was surprised to see Hatem among the diving children. He too was bare-chested and holding a watermelon to his waist. Hatem, his best friend with the dirty skin of a freewheeling troublemaker, a loudmouth whose face was crisscrossed with scars that testified to daring feats. The opposite of Rami, who was very white and too skinny and whose shyness clung to every part of him.

"Look, my little lizard! Watch this!"

Lizard was a nickname given to weaklings.

Two seconds ticked by and then Hatem's body slammed into the water and disappeared. The other children may have taken a good ten seconds to resurface but the seconds Hatem took seemed to last for minutes. Rami counted. Rami had always counted.

From the age of three he had shut himself away in his own world. He wasn't interested in other people, but played alone in a corner and stared constantly at the pendulum on the clock that had pride of place in the living room. He never looked up when someone spoke to him. As if he were just another object. Until the day when, out of nowhere, he'd decided to open his mouth. Not to say "Mommy" or "Daddy" but to reel off a sequence of numbers while pointing at the living-room clock whose mystery he'd deciphered. Sounding almost boastful, he'd started counting out loud, to his mother's delight. Unable to believe her ears, Muhja had even shrieked with glee: "*Abqari*! My son's an *abqari*! Ahmed, come and see, your son's a genius!" His father, who never smiled, had smiled. Rami had never stopped counting since.

Gasping for breath, the intrepid Hatem eventually popped his head back out of the Euphrates to applause from the crowd. The watermelon had been well and truly buried. Turning to look at Rami, he roared and brandished a fist. Rami raised his in reply but didn't dare shout, afraid of attracting attention. Talking, laughing, yelling—that wasn't what he was here for. He'd come to forget the black she-wolves' voices that were still ringing inside his head.

Hatem had already initiated Rami into all sorts of rituals. Rituals to "make men of them," such as their first shared cigarette, or the pebbles they threw at shopwindows, and then there was the hunt for lethal scorpions that hadn't ended well. For Hatem, rituals ratified a pact of loyalty. And on this day, hardly surprisingly, he once again encouraged Rami to make a man of himself. Hatem exercised considerable influence over his protégé, so it was only natural that Rami ended up on the bridge.

"In Fallujah becoming a man means taking on the Euphrates, my little lizard."

Rami straightened up and stood tall on the ledge, alongside the diving children who sized him up and could smell his fear. Sure, two seconds wasn't much on a clock. But in life it was a whole different story. It was all about the before—the extremely high risk, or at least the pain, the suffering—to then emerge rinsed, cleansed, gleaming. From such a height, there was no room for error. This perfect margin would surely help you to come to terms with yourself, alone, confronting the void, a metaphor for life and death. Escaping, feeling humbled in the face of such emptiness. Rami wanted to experience this magical state.

Sounding like a protective older brother, Hatem encouraged him. "You, Rami, are going to jump like all the others who deserve to be called men. And you're going to bury that watermelon."

Burying a watermelon at the bottom of the river was a trial of strength, a rite of passage, an ode to courage. The Euphrates was known for its treachery, its strong current, and its whirlpools. Learning to swim in it was a feat in itself; burying such a heavy piece of fruit in its bed when you couldn't swim was madness.

The other children started to lose interest. Hatem grew impatient. Rami needed to jump. His reputation would have an impact on Hatem's.

"Look down and jump!" Hatem urged his baulking friend. "Don't think about it!"

Rami followed the older boy's advice. Suddenly thoughtful, he looked up and stared at the sky, hiding his fear. Isn't that what courage is? Overcoming your fears. And wasn't overcoming your fears living? He needed to stop thinking. And stop backing down. The tension built gradually as the other children's voices joined Hatem's.

"Come on, Rami, you can do it! Go on! Jump!"

No way to back out. He just needed to launch himself without thinking about anything. Dressed in long white shorts that afforded only glimpses of his thin calves, Rami trembled as he stepped toward the edge. He closed his eyes before letting himself drop into emptiness. Those two seconds seemed far bulkier, he could feel time loosening until his body kissed the water to shouts from Hatem and his gang.

Suddenly alone in the silence of the depths, Rami wondered whether he'd found the exact locus of the strange attraction that the Euphrates exercised over him, the ideal place to stop hearing those shrill voices. As if instinctively responding to his grim torment, as if the river were saying no, Rami's body rose upward of its own accord, searching for the tiniest vital parcel of air. He gathered his wits again thanks to Hatem's encouragement. Rami could see his friend gesticulating up there on the bridge, most likely giving him instructions that he couldn't hear. Was he telling him to avoid making any sudden moves? Did Hatem know Rami couldn't swim? The older boy could jump up and down as much as he liked, it wouldn't change anything. Rami and his watermelon were still stuck in the middle of the Euphrates.

All at once everything accelerated. Rami was caught up in one of those famous whirlpools and he started writhing in every direction. Submerged in terror, sucked back into the river's belly, he paddled with all his might, using his arms, his legs, and his despair. With every breath interrupted by the water, Rami took in mouthfuls of the Euphrates, aware of his heart racing and his lungs screaming. He could no longer hear Hatem's cries nor the litany of the black she-wolves. Where exactly was courage? Had he finally become a man? He started looking for the bridge to set himself a goal, but it swiftly vanished from his field of vision. When he lost all sense of direction his whole short life flashed before his eyes. A life spent surrounded by siblings of whom he was the youngest, with a taciturn father and a mother in precarious health.

Rami's mother was a sweetly, naively good woman. She had blue eyes and a face with an opalescent beauty and an extreme pallor that contrasted with her black hair. Her frail body, sapped by years of illness, miraculously managed to keep its balance. Rami had always known his mother as bedridden and in pain, but loving. A too-young sickly patient whom he adored with a child's love. Ahmed, his father, was a glum, withdrawn man with a generous mouth and a pointed nose that appeared to battle with gravity.

While the Euphrates tried to drown Rami by drawing him to the depths, his two brothers' faces loomed into his mind's eye. Tarek and Khaled.

Tarek's blue eyes, his fair hair and stocky body, his voice already gravelly from a few years of rolled tobacco. Khaled, the eldest, a more silent, dreamy, and spiritual sort with a gentle voice and a faraway look, far from this lowly earth and from Rami's world.

The Euphrates was now just a wild sea that wanted to be done with him. Rami struggled to stay alive. In the heat of combat with this aquatic ogre, at the heart of his visions, another apparition emerged: his mother. Muhja and her Rami in the *iwan*, an open-plan space typical of most Iraqi homes. The most comfortable spot, the central room. The *iwan* connected the whole house. It opened onto the garden but also the kitchen, the bedrooms, and the stone staircase to the roof and the chicken coop. He remembered nights when he and his mother gazed at the sky, watched shooting stars, listened to donkeys braying and wolves howling. Wild nights that left Fallujah at the mercy of the desert. Then those first glimmers of dawn when Rami and Muhja woke with the hierarchical orchestra of the natural world around them, led by the rooster. Next came the refrain from the henhouse, the call of the muezzin, and closing the ceremony came the crackle of the transistor radio clamped to his father's ear. The members of Rami's family were very different, but, just like Muhja, they miraculously kept in balance.

With every lungful of water Rami could feel death hovering over his soul. The Euphrates gave him no respite now. In the middle of one of his final visions, he saw Muhja smiling at him, Muhja running her hands through his hair, Muhja quietly singing a strange litany to him. Then all of a sudden darkness, silence, oblivion.

A few minutes later, or a few centuries—Rami couldn't be sure—he felt a powerful hand shaking him. He came to lying on the damp mud beside the river. Hatem was looking at him, peering over him with a smile.

"Welcome to the world of men, my little lizard!"

Rami hadn't hesitated before diving in even though he couldn't swim. Had he wanted to die? Well, he'd fought to survive. So he hadn't meant to end it all but rather to eliminate a part of himself, Hatem was sure of it. What was it he wanted to kill? Hatem reached out a hand to him.

"Talk to me, Rami. You can always rely on me, my friend," he said quietly, helping him up.

Still dazed by the Euphrates and trying to pull himself together, Rami gave a sharp yowl. The unbearable voices from earlier that sorrowful morning were coming to life in him. Hatem begged his friend to confide in him, to tell him what was going on. Rami started to cry, blocked his ears to stop hearing the voices, then closed his eyes to the scene of horror.

"Yaboooooo! Yabooooooooooooooooo!"

Women's shrill wails had torn through the gloom of Fallujah's dawn. The air had become denser, time had stood still. At first, Rami had thought it was wolves howling, circling him in his nightmare. Through the doorway that separated his bedroom from the *iwan*, he'd seen the black-clad mourners. These daybreak she-wolves were mourning a death and making sure everyone knew. Rami had only had to listen and he'd recognized death. The black she-wolves had howled to honor Muhja's memory. Shudders had run up and down Rami's body. Those voices, which were as beautiful as they were terrifying, had pierced his heart.

And now he understood.

His mother was lying on a thin mattress on the ground. Her hair was the color of wet mud after it has rained over Fallujah. Her skin looked like the sky yellowed by the *asifa*, the sandstorms that regularly swept through the city. Eyes closed, lips tightly shut, nose pinched, Muhja looked as if she was sleeping.

But her heart had stopped beating. She'd stopped breathing.

Rami had recognized her, but it was no longer her. She was now just an inert body surrounded by official mourners and their lamentations. Rami had seen his father, silent, dry-eyed, apparently cut off from the world; and then Tarek in tears; Khaled wasn't there. He absolutely had to get out. Skirt around the three women. Leave the house. Spend time alone by the river. Escape. No, he hadn't dreamed it. This nightmare had opened his eyes to the death of the person who meant the most to him.

That was why Rami had taken refuge by the Euphrates and why he'd withdrawn into the garden of his inner landscape, shielded from watching eyes, far from the turmoil. Despair had driven him to jump off the bridge. It wasn't courage that had propelled him but the temptation of ending it all. And then Muhja's voice had come to him. She was humming the chorus of a poem that was popular in Fallujah, blocking out the cries of the she-wolves who had come to fetch her. *Momma, I crossed the Euphrates for you. I put you on my head and swam to drown your wounds.*

Drown her wounds. That's what Rami had tried to do. Muhja had known that death lived under her roof, that it would come knocking sooner than anticipated, so she'd sung for Rami.

That song had come back to him like a refrain while he thought he was dying in the river. He'd sung it so he could join Muhja, but he'd survived. From now on Rami's mornings wouldn't sing, only the silence left by this abyssal maternal absence would grow inside him. Rami wasn't dead, but didn't losing your mother mean losing your life?

It was customary in Fallujah to use hired mourners, she-wolves dressed in black, to wail on behalf of other people, therefore preserving the propriety of those who were suffering in silence.

On that morning, on the edge of the river and the edge of death, Rami tried to find another mainstay, a different miracle that would allow him to keep his balance.

ROOM 219

(August 3, 2019)

EUPHRATES. I bear the name of the thing that could have killed my father.

And on that August day, it felt as if I was hearing about it for the first time.

Had he never told me this drowning story in order to protect me? Would my name have been too heavy to bear? How would I have taken it if I'd known what it meant to him?

Being woken by those wails announcing a death, losing his mother so young, almost drowning—my father's first memories helped me gauge how lucky I was to have both my parents still. Like Rami, I'd had a phobia of water as a child. A phobia it had been hard to shake thanks to a gym teacher who'd pushed me off a diving board. I'd been the same age as Rami had been when he jumped from the green bridge. I almost drowned and was fished out of the pool with a long pole just in time. I felt humiliated. This betrayal forced me to confront my fear and put my trust in no one but myself. So I decided to learn to swim because I no longer had faith in anyone else.

————

That faith was tested again during my father's very first consultation. Before he was told he had cancer, he was transferred to a diagnostic center, a specialized lung clinic, for as long as it took to identify the source of the problem. The place looked like an old school with plaster crumbling off the walls and long, oppressive corridors. It oozed end of life.

Three weeks of tests and pulmonary drains, of shuttling between doctors, specialists, a physiotherapist who massaged his swollen legs and listened impassively to his complaining, and two young nurses who unloaded their own professional burnout onto their patients. On the first day the specialist proved reassuring. Despite the greenish tinge to my father's face, it was "not too serious." At best, a lung infection or a recalcitrant bacterium. At worst, pneumonia. Very common in smokers, he said. A few days' rest, and he could go home. Had he been smoking long?

"Since the revolution in 1958!" my father said with a twinkle.

An embarrassed laugh from the doctor, who couldn't really place the revolution mentioned by the *very nice* Mr. Ahmed.

I was relieved.

———

It all turned on its head the next day. The word "shadow" came and darkened our relief. Very quickly—too quickly—the serious implications of his illness had found their way back in. Shadow. A word that opened the door to other, more threatening ones that I would have preferred never to hear. They lined up one after the other to slither down the ill-judged slope of my denial. Now things were "very serious." The tone of voice, the evasive eyes, and the choice of words added up to a definitive diagnosis. Tumor. Malignant. Lung. Advanced. Second tumor. Stage IV. Metastasized. All that was missing was the word *death*. The doctor wore an ersatz reassuring smile. How could anyone smile as they announced another person's imminent death? And there was one thing he'd said that I'll never forget: *But still, there is some hope.*

That *but still* meant *it's over.*

A hand on his shoulder would have been less deceitful. The doctor had just sacrificed the truth on the altar of my own hopes.

I stayed standing to avoid collapsing completely. I wanted to disappear, to escape this new reality. My father was sitting between those two words, trapped between the *but* and the *still*, his eyes trailing from me to the doctor who closed the door to the room with one last lie: "Mr. Ahmed, we're going to transfer you to the Bizet Clinic to treat your cancer. Don't worry, it will all be fine."

"So, what did he say?" my father asked after the doctor had left. "When do I get out?"

He may well have been deaf in one ear and losing his French for the last few years, but on that particular day my father was pretending not to understand. I'm still convinced of that.

I looked at him for a moment, which felt as long as a boring summer, and didn't admit my terror, then I muttered the words *tumor* and *treatment* with a pretense of normality, before reminding him that the doctor had said there was hope. Yes, that wild hope we cling to when all is lost. Whatever is the point of it if not for us to believe and therefore to doubt? I tried to cleanse the word of the dirty reality that had just been spattered over it. My father looked at me but didn't reply. His eyes said: If you want to trick death and pretend to live, hope is pointless.

———————

The day after that conversation I visited my father in room 219 at the Bizet Clinic. I was still his son up until the wretched day, August 2, 2019, when denial of the first illness gave way to the second. Cancer and amnesia battled it out continuously. My mother and sister came into the room a few minutes after my conversation with the good lord doctor. My father didn't recognize them. I explained everything. That the doctor had said we should tread gently, we mustn't overburden him with too many faces, that I was his first point of reference so it fell to me to manage what happened next, that I would be the only one to see him for a while, and we'd have to be patient. My mother and sister left room 219 in tears. My father was the world to my mother—a husband and a father. She'd never had a father of her own and had learned everything from him. Starting with how to cook. All through my childhood, I'd heard him gently correcting her when she was making our favorite dish, kubba halab, a sort of rice dumpling stuffed with minced meat flavored with parsley.

"Wafa, you really need to squidge the rice with your hands, you mustn't let any air in or the kubba will fall apart."

My father loved demonstrating this technique to us.

Once his memory started falling apart too, I was the one short of air. I no longer really knew who I was to him. Facing him alone, I became aware of my new responsibility. Every sentence, every word, every detail would matter. I was also worried that I might capsize his new reality by talking about mine.

Only a few days before his cancer was identified, I'd brought an end to my marriage. I hadn't dared tell him. His illness had already been there. That tragedy was enough in itself. Mine was insignificant. Only my mother and sister knew. I wanted to spare my father any notion of failure. In his mind, failure spoke of a quite different color, a buried pain, a distant nightmare. I discovered later that my mother, who was incapable of hiding anything from her husband, had told him my secret just before the amnesia struck. My father had replied: *Luckily, there aren't any children.* Thinking over it now, the signs already pointed to a change in his memory. Amnesia was budding inside him and I had no idea—unlike my mother. To think I believed I was sparing her when she was the one protecting me. And all that time when I saw him every day, he knew about my marriage. Was he waiting for me to raise the subject?

Now he'd forgotten everything, and I was shamefully relieved.

"Do you still know who I am, Dad?"

"You're my son. I have a daughter and a wife. I have a family."

"In order to keep going, the traveler needs to jettison bad memories and bad experiences from the suitcase so he can still carry it," I ventured.

My father didn't react. He just looked at me quizzically.

"You told me that quite a few times when I asked you questions as a child."

"I did? It doesn't mean a thing to me."

With his amnesia, I witnessed the death of my "before" father. My "after" father had lost whole swathes of his life story, names, dates, and faces. Even the invisible suitcase.

"I often asked you who I was and where I was from."

"But you know who you are, I'm the one who's forgotten, right?"

I was struck by this retort.

"Yes, Dad, I know who I am."

He said nothing for a moment.

"Tell me who I was when I was me."

The irony of this situation was a cruel mirror image of my childhood questions. Thirty years on, the question that had obsessed me as a child was being asked again, but the other way around.

"Okay, I'll tell you who you were, who my father was."

I thought it might help him retrieve his memory. We would improvise a verbal jousting match of memories and see ourselves in a new light. I didn't know what it felt like no longer being able to describe a life or whether I should protect him from the world he'd forgotten. What merit was there in saying nothing when confronted with the pain of having forgotten so much? For my father, wouldn't remembering feel like being hauled from the Euphrates again, as Hatem had done? The conversation I'd always hoped for was right there, and it was calling to me. If we were to retrace our lives after the forgetting set in, should I opt for light or darkness? Should I shy away from nuanced details, from pain, upheavals, and mistakes? Focus only on happiness and cloudless skies? Choose between happiness and unhappiness, life's mismatched twins? Should I delve through blind spots? And, above all, how was I to piece together the fragments he'd left to me? I read somewhere that trauma could be passed on from generation to generation, that studies on survivors of genocide had confirmed evidence of genetic modifications, an imprint of the horrors individuals had experienced in their DNA, trauma tattooed under their skin, and it could be handed down to their descendants. What about orphans? Could the feeling of abandonment buried deep inside them also be passed on?

My father would tell me about his childhood, and I would tell him part of mine. Taking up the reins myself wasn't going to be easy, but this quid pro quo felt essential. I didn't want to reel off words as if stringing beads, or picking at wounds. Well, perhaps I did. By the very nature of things, I had the choice. He did not. But, and this was what really mattered, he was agreeing to open his invisible suitcase. And so I opened mine.

I'M YOUR SON,
YOU HAVE A DAUGHTER
AND A WIFE. YOU HAVE A FAMILY.

(Fall 1987)

DEATH CAME into my life when I was seven years old, in the form of a synonym: deceased. In our working-class neighborhood a lot of people were affected by the scourge of the heroin years. As children, my sister and I often played in the sandbox surrounded by used syringes.

On this particular day, the young man was lying nearby with a small, whitish syringe stuck into his thigh. One of the paramedics who'd come to take him away didn't bother with precautions that might spare us the macabre facts of the scene.

"Deceased," he yelled.

There were constellations of blue blotches on the victim's face and skinny arms. I was too young for this blue death, and I've never forgotten it. It kept me awake at night for months. Then the insomnia gave way to my existential questions: What are life and death? What are we doing here and who are we? Not that I really understood why I felt this need to wonder about these things. And yet I knew where it stemmed from: I was terrified by the thought of dying like that anonymous man abandoned by the sandbox. Since my earliest childhood I've always felt invisible, alone, directionless, an outside observer of my own life, with an inexplicable feeling of unease.

That was when I stopped going out to play. I was afraid of the outside world because of that inert body I'd seen. So I spent my Sundays at home.

I liked Sundays. They followed an unchanging pattern: My mother did the housework and my father went to the market. Since the episode with the corpse, my father had stopped asking me to go with him. My sister went instead. I stayed home with my mother, who methodically dusted the furniture, cleaned the carpets, and wiped down the fridge. She left the closets till last every time.

I've always been drawn to the backs of closets. I liked cutting myself off from the world, inhaling the tang of mothballs, the smell of slow-moving time, wafts of the past. In among the well-worn clothes, I often came across forgotten old things. A battered sewing machine, a book with a torn cover, a crumbling leather belt. These abandoned vestiges had no hope of being reclaimed, and I liked touching them and smelling them, then giving my imagination free rein. Had they had a moment of glory? Perhaps the sewing machine had been used to patch together a wedding dress, the book had made someone change their opinion, and the leather belt had been tightened around someone's gut, saving their dignity. I could spend hours bringing them back to life, like a pirate child in search of forgotten treasure.

One snowy Sunday when the ground was cold and the sky white, I made an interesting discovery: a sturdy brown leather briefcase with a combination lock set on the numerals 7, 5, 8. I'd never seen it before. I squeezed the two clasps and, to my surprise, the briefcase creaked open. It was the right combination. The case smelled musty. Inside it, I found a roll of negatives in a little canister. I unwound it straightaway and took it over to the window to study the images.

In the first one I recognized my parents wearing bell-bottoms, with long hair and square sunglasses. In the second, Bibi Nahda, my maternal grandmother, elegant in a long dress. My mother had told me a lot about her and shown me photos in which she reached out her arms toward me. She'd visited us in the past, but I'd been too young to remember. My mother claimed my father adored her: They could talk politics together—Bibi Nahda was one of the few Iraqi women who'd been to a university in the 1940s. I would have loved to have known her, but sadly my grandmother left this world too soon, surrounded by her books. I don't remember feeling anything, apart from my mother's grief; she cried for days on end. Bibi Nahda died right in the middle of the Iran-Iraq War. The country's borders were closed so my mother couldn't attend the burial.

Other pictures showed my parents with a group of friends in stripy, hand-knit sweaters, picking flowers in the fields. A concentrate of the 1970s in sepia monochrome tinged with carefree spirit. Try as I might to find my father's family in all those negatives, they simply didn't feature. Not one photo of his parents, nor of an uncle or aunt. I may not have met my mother's family, but at least I'd seen photos of them. On my father's side, nothing.

Continuing my exploration of the briefcase, I spotted a plastic bag in an inner pocket. Inside it I found documents and more photos. One of these immediately grabbed my attention: a black-and-white portrait of a young man sitting on a wooden chair and staring so intently at the lens that I felt he was in the room with me. His crooked smile made him look slightly teasing. His gentle face and angular, beardless chin accentuated how young he was—probably around twenty. He was wearing an immaculate military uniform with a narrow black tie around his neck, and he had his legs crossed. His right hand rested on his left, drawing attention to a handsome watch with a black leather strap, a silver case, and three small white dials. The athletic-looking young man held himself upright but with an air of nonchalance. A perfect pose, which accentuated his charisma. When I looked more closely, I recognized him.

It was my father.

I'd never seen him so young, so slim, and so self-assured. I carried on delving into the past and came across a small, yellowed ID photo stapled to a little card. In the spaces for first name and family name, written in both Arabic and English: Amir Mullah. I didn't immediately understand what I was reading. My father was called Rami, not Amir. Caught between fear and a sense of betrayal, I felt my heart rate quicken. This was definitely my father, but the name on the card wasn't his. I slipped the photo into my pocket, determined to confront him with my find as soon as he was home from the market. Continuing with my investigations, I spotted a billfold full of business cards. One of them had a red logo on it with two crossed tools—a hammer and sickle. On the back were a few words in Arabic. I closed the briefcase with no idea what exactly I'd unearthed. I just knew there was a story hiding behind that photo and the ID card with the unfamiliar name on it.

I held out that image yellowed by the years to my mother, who was busying away in the kitchen.

"This is Dad, right?"

She looked up, then, without taking her eyes off the photo, she sat down, obviously as surprised as I was.

She sat in silence for a long while before pinching her upper lip—something she always did when she was anxious. Usually such a cheerful woman, she now seemed sad. Her smile had vanished. Something was wrong.

"Have to ask your father," she said, returning to her chores.

My father. He wasn't like other fathers. He didn't have a car, didn't go to an office, didn't wear a tie. I didn't know much about his life, apart from when and where he was born: January 25, 1944, in Fallujah. What had his childhood been like? I had no idea. I imagined his youth spent

amid the golden dunes of a vast desert, alongside dromedaries, Bedouins pouring tea, and genies emerging from
lamps.

I myself was born in France in 1980, a catastrophic
year, the year the Iran-Iraq War began. That war marked
out my childhood before I could even understand why.
Before it, Iraq hadn't existed as far as I was concerned,
except at breakfast time when it came to us thanks to
the family radio tuned to Radio Orient. I knew the fre-
quency it was on, 94.3, and its jingle by heart. The news
constantly reminded me that I was not allowed to see
this country. Apparently, it was because of Khomeini and
Saddam—two men who despised each other and whom
my father loathed just as much. Whenever he heard their
names on the radio, he would spit and call them *abna el
kilab*—sons of dogs. For a long time, I thought that being
Iraqi meant not saying very much and spitting when you
weren't happy about something. So I took to imitating
Dad when he wasn't there. I learned the swear words and
spluttered at the TV or the radio in order to be as Iraqi
as he was.

My sister and I were the result of an unplanned meeting between an exiled student and a beautiful young tour-
ist from the same country who could no longer cope with
the furnace of Iraqi summers. My mother, who was young
and carefree, was as pretty as springtime. The day that
Wafa met Rami, a terrible bout of toothache had stopped
her from uttering a single word. But when she looked into

the eyes of that young man with the shoulder-length hair, a redemptive breath of air eased her pain and she started talking again. I knew this story inside out but no more than that: two foreigners a long way from Iraq, clearly happy and filled with hope for the lives that lay ahead of them. My mother had described this life-changing chance encounter many times as she turned the pages of the family album. But there was always something missing. The album contained photos only of my mother and her family. The ones of my father didn't start until he was an adult, as if his earlier life had never existed.

I knew that here, in France, he devoted his life to supporting us. Every last bit of money he earned he entrusted to my mother to ask forgiveness for unkept promises. For a long time, all we'd known were insecurity, need, and a sometimes-empty fridge. Rami and Wafa often fought about unpaid bills and burdensome silences. My father took loans from friends. I once caught him making a phone call to a "friend" whose name and very existence were news to me. Having snuck behind him, I eavesdropped on the conversation with the phone's handset pressed hard against my ear. It was a brief exchange.

"Yes, my friend, I can lend you a thousand francs if you like," an amicable voice said in the end.

"Why was the man talking about a thousand francs?" I asked.

I remember to this day the flush of red on my father's face.

He replied with a smile that wasn't really a smile. And from that day forward he would be out of the house during the day.

Our childhood was like a lead weight hanging by a thread, maintained by short-lived casual jobs. Window cleaner, warehouse janitor, newspaper salesman outside the Métro station. My father muddled along for better or worse, or for worse or better. And then one day he was offered different work, still on the street but more lucrative.

Once he started earning regularly, he came home in the evenings and put his black leather bag down on the coffee table in the living room. It was filled with currencies from all over the world: yen, dollars, deutschmarks, pounds sterling, Italian lira. My sister and I would sort, count and count again, laying out wads by nationality and totting up his long day's takings. We thought it was fun, and I think he was proud to be earning all this money with the sweat of his brow.

My father wasn't traveling around the world; the world was coming to him. He paced up and down on the paving stones outside Notre-Dame de Paris every day, selling postcards to tourists. In the evenings, he came home exhausted, sat down in "his" chair, as silent as ever, with a few carrot sticks and radishes, a bottle of beer, and his Walkman headset over his ears. We were not to disturb him, not to ask the wrong question, not to wake the dormant volcano.

We had a roof over our heads but were only one step away from being shown the door. The bailiffs reminded us of this regularly with their letters and threats and seals. So we moved a lot. We had no ties. We lost our friends with every move. At the time, the world was vast. Leaving a city was like changing countries. We could live ten kilometers from previous friends and never bump into them.

Despite all this, we were a stable family unit: my parents; my younger sister, Arwa, who was named after a distant queen; and me. We lived in a small apartment in the suburbs of Paris, on the first floor of a white building with crumbling plaster. It was on the edge of Les Tilleuls projects—a fancy name evoking linden trees but there wasn't a single linden tree to be seen. The only sample of nature was to be found on the one road that led out of the housing project, lined with tall, dancing poplar trees.

We were in an urban development zone, opposite a freight station. I went to sleep every evening lulled by the endless convoys of freight trains that made my bed pitch. This dormitory town was just a staging post, no one ever stayed there long. Just like the trains, we were in transit.

I liked that apartment, despite the fact its kitchen overlooked a grayish cemetery and never wearied of reminding us, from the moment we sat down to breakfast, that the dimming light of evening wasn't far away and someday life would end there, among the tombstones.

———————

The market emptied of people at about one o'clock. At lunchtime, I heard my father's footsteps on the stairs. I was set on getting things straight, dusting down the obscure portrait of a father who never talked about his childhood and who swore by silence alone. I was eager to find out more about this man who never mentioned his country. When my friends told me about their vacations in the countryside or their grandparents' war stories, I had no anecdotes to offer. Would that black-and-white photo found in an old plastic bag fill in the blanks?

During lunch, an insidious unease settled over the kitchen, the tension of a family secret about to be unmasked. My father looked away.

"What do you want to know?" he asked.

I took the photo from my pocket. "Why are you dressed like a soldier?"

He barely glanced at it. "I did my national service. It was compulsory in Iraq. Like in France."

"And why's your name different on here?" I persisted, brandishing the card. My voice cracked, betraying my emotion.

My mother poured a glass of milk for my sister. I was obstinately hoping to be served up a bit of truth instead. I waited, motionless. My mother poured a glass for me in turn. I kept my arms crossed. I wanted to know everything. Immediately.

"Things aren't always what they seem, Euphrates," my father replied eventually in the same solemn voice he used for my bad report cards. He was still looking away.

"Will you tell me about it?"

"You're too young, there are things it's better not to know at your age. Someday, maybe, I'll tell you. It's too complicated."

It's too complicated. Period. His way of avoiding the subject.

I didn't finish my food that evening either. I was upset, frustrated.

My mother came to see me at bedtime and made a point of closing the door behind her. She sat down on the edge of my bed and I kept up my questions, but she knew little more than I did.

"All families have a secret, you know, *habibi.* Your father was somebody," she confided. "If you want him to talk, be patient, he may one day."

My father *was.* She was talking about him in the past tense. Who *was* he?

I couldn't understand my father's reluctance to tell me about his past. He'd always been there with us without being completely there. With that way he had of looking up at the ceiling or the sky when he drew on a cigarette, then sighing out the smoke to form a gray cloud which hid an unsuspected world full of silences and *It's too complicated.*

Complicated. I heard the word so much I hated it. It was an accumulation of refusal, failure, and withdrawal. It seemed absurd. Did I need to get older to understand? The real point of the word *complicated* was to say nothing, to avoid as much contact as possible.

With time I worked at simplifying life's issues, explaining them, understanding them, and describing them, because everything was too *complicated*. I had grasped one thing: Where my father complicated things, I liked to simplify. That was why I was so determined to make him talk, to get to know the man who was making his own life a misery every day so that I could make a success of mine.

SAMIYA

(Summer 1953)

FALLUJAH WAS a town between two worlds, a pretty little place full of contradictions and paradoxes. It stood on the edge of the Euphrates in a fertile valley and was surrounded by plum-colored sand in summer. It was sometimes peaceful, sometimes noisy, neither too close to nor too far from the excitements of Baghdad, and the scent of flowers that hung in the air was often replaced by the strong smell of mule dung around a street corner. In terms of architecture, Fallujah was typical of western Iraqi villages with its millennial date palms, its covered markets and clay-colored houses. In actual fact it was the very definition of antagonism. The city-slicker women without veils eyed the village types dressed head to toe in black. Pretty bungalows turned up their noses at impoverished back alleys. And main roads paraded all the smugness of the nouveaux riches, gawped at by people who turned their backs on the town every evening and rode home on their donkeys, proudly carrying all the dignity and destitution of poverty.

———

After Muhja's death, Rami stopped talking. At night, his brother Tarek would sometimes hear him sobbing in a corner of the bedroom that they shared with their eldest brother, Khaled. How does a child survive without his mother? How does he live with other people when every day and night constantly remind him of this great sorrow?

A year of mourning had elapsed when clouds darkened Rami's skies once more. In Iraqi culture, a whole year had to pass before society deemed the amount of mourning acceptable. A year for the pain to undergo its transformation, sloughing off its prickly carapace and becoming no more than a bad memory. A century wouldn't have been long enough for Rami. But his father, Ahmed, already wanted to remarry. Local custom suggested that a widower should marry one of his late wife's sisters if need be, to maintain the blood ties and safeguard the continuation of a mother's upbringing. Ahmed was looking for a strong woman, someone who'd be able to run his home. He asked for the hand of one of Muhja's sisters, a woman whom Rami had seen only once in his life and who appeared to be in good health.

Muhja's parents refused.

After raking through relations, Ahmed settled for Samiya, a woman who had also been widowed, a mother of three who'd never lived in a town or had a peaceful life. Fallujah and the surrounding villages were emerging from an insurrection against British forces. Even though the Hashemite Kingdom of Iraq had been independent since 1932, it was still under the thumb of Her Majesty's soldiers. King Faisal, who had been enthroned by the former English occupiers, proved incapable of bridging the gap between the extreme opulence of the few and the acute poverty of everyone else—those who lived around Fallujah. In these small towns, there were rumblings of opposition to the British occupation and the kingdom. English troops and Iraqi loyalists were regularly ambushed by Iraqi tribes, particularly from the village of Garma, where Ahmed's new wife, Samiya, lived. Rumor was that she'd joined in the fight, stolen munitions from the British troops' arms depot, and spat at British soldiers in the street. And they were quick to throw insults at her in return.

"Witch! *Kelba*! Waster!"

Witch, dog, waster—terms that persisted when the bullets fell silent, and were then appropriated by local Iraqis.

So Samiya left a world of insults, military boots, and village warfare to marry a town dweller who, like her, was widowed but seemed overwhelmed by life.

When Rami first met Samiya, he didn't know how to behave around her—she was physically so different from Muhja: tall, slender, dressed in a black abaya, unsmiling. And she watched Rami closely, severely. Her eyes were very dark, set deep in an ill-tempered face, and her thin arms were as angular as the green tribal tattoo on her chin. Her first, deceptively gentle words to him were freighted with menace.

"Go fetch me a glass of water."

From that day forward, Samiya monitored Rami's every action, his every move, and she started forbidding him everything. He succumbed to profound anxiety and a sense of foreboding the more his stepmother favored her own children: Saad, Ayad, and Riyad. She rejected Rami and leapt at any tiny opportunity to accuse him of wrongdoing, publicly humiliate him, or privately insult him.

According to tradition, having a stepmother in the household should have protected Rami. Instead, he paid the price for an absurd, unfair, and destructive jealousy. The whole neighborhood nostalgically paid tribute to Muhja while Samiya was merely a second wife, a simple village woman, the last thread in the fabric of Iraqi society.

With the passing months, Rami became the innocent victim of this posthumous female rivalry. Samiya's status as a second wife coupled with the impossibility of reaching out to Rami with an innate love engendered the opposite emotion in her, a sort of aversion for the son of the beautiful blue-eyed city girl. Rami hadn't experienced the British occupation, but Samiya and her children became occupiers in his own life, his territory now bereft of a queen: his childhood.

After Muhja's death, the river was his only refuge, and Hatem seemed like the dawn light in the shadows cast by Samiya. Rami ran off to meet his friend every day, narrowly missing carts blocking access to the bridge so that he could join the other children at the far end. Escaping to the river was the one peaceful break he could grant himself. Away from the thunderbolts disrupting his new household.

Fallujah was stripped of everything and had no real infrastructure. The emblematic bridge, a gift from the British, was the town's only attraction, a magnet for street children. This metal monster, painted green and rising to about fifteen meters, meant that people could now cross from one bank to the other on foot, riding a donkey, or by car. The outlying villages had drawn closer to the town center. Townspeople and rural folks mingled there every day.

Since Rami had undertaken his ritual jump, the children at the bridge had stopped sneering at him. Now able to bury watermelons in the silt and bring them back up in the evening, he had joined the ranks of the risk-takers and shrugged off his former shyness like an old skin. Rami had been certified. And Hatem was proud to have been a part of the process. Hatem was the only person in whom Rami occasionally dared to confide.

"Is that snake still chasing you?"

"She insults me. She rejects me. She hates me…"

She. He never mentioned her name.

He described bullying, humiliation, and the storm-laden sky that permanently hung over him.

She whose children went to school in new warm clothes in winter, while he was allowed only one item of clothing and a pair of sandals. She who, when he took to wetting the bed almost every night, raced out to brandish his sheets in the street at dawn, yelling to anyone who'd listen that this was the work of "the other woman's child." Rami was well aware of the mocking chuckles and stifled laughter. Hatem knew about his friend's purgatory and always found the right thing to say.

"Be patient, my little lizard. If there is a God, she'll be punished! No one should mistreat a *yatim*. Remember the good times in the past with your mother, remember her, and this other woman won't be able to get to you."

Yatim. Rami was now motherless. And over the last few months he'd battled to remember that. At home, Muhja's gentle voice had given way to Samiya's shrill exclamations.

"What about your father, doesn't he say anything?"

Rami didn't reply. He left the question dangling. No, his father didn't say anything. He was distant, hard, irritable, and authoritarian. Although he had occasional flashes of temper, he mostly said nothing. The rare moments of levity from Muhja's time had vanished. In fact, Rami wondered whether he'd ever seen his father smile, granting other people that curve of the lips that reconciles things.

"Shit, my father! I have to go! See you later," Rami muttered, hastily leaving his friend.

Yes, he was meant to be meeting this father who despised lateness. Three times a week, Ahmed went to the souk and drafted letters and legal documents for people who couldn't write. In the market, he was a respectable man, a public writer greeted and in demand on every street corner. His whole being resided in that market. Its noises and smells smothered his complaining and silences at home. As Rami made his way there, he wondered why, at home, his father was a shadow of his true self, nothing but a ghost with rainy-day eyes.

Had a part of him died with Muhja? Samiya sucked the air out of everything around her, and held sway over him, at Rami's expense. The smallest misstep made by one of her "real" children was always transferred onto her wretched stepson. This injustice, which crept insidiously into Rami's day-to-day existence, forged his silence. He never complained at home, not to his brothers nor his father who was blind to his suffering anyway. The man even allowed his new wife to commit this abuse right under his nose. But did he even see it?

In the evenings, Samiya had instilled a sort of hierarchy. She and her husband ate first, then her children, then Ahmed's two older boys, Khaled and Tarek, and lastly Rami, who was allowed what was left over. All household chores were saved for him. The dishes, cleaning the bathrooms, the henhouse. Rami needed to learn, she said. In fact, Samiya's orders succeeded in breaking him mentally, burning out what was left of his mother in him, and scattering the still-warm ashes. And no one protested.

One day when Samiya wouldn't stop bullying him, tears of exhaustion and rage started to roll down Rami's cheeks. And he protested for the first time, in front of everyone.

"I'm just a child! Leave me alone!"

Rami was granted just one icy retort full of contempt: "You're nothing."

He reeled at the insult. Nothing. A word to crack his skull, cloud his vision, annihilate him.

His father didn't look up. His brothers said nothing.

Samiya had decided to destroy Rami. And no one stopped her.

The next day, in response to Rami's outrageous disobedience, Samiya decreed that the other woman's children would have to work to contribute to household funds. Rami and Tarek would sell kleichas, little cookies—that she would make—filled with dates and cardamom. How could she cook something so sweet and delicious? Rami wondered. Khaled, the eldest, was spared this task. With his father's support, he had joined a group of students in one of the town's mosques to study Sufi Islam and pursue a family tradition handed from father to son. To become an imam, live in his own mosque, and perpetuate the lineage which, according to the legend of their paternal line (and a preciously preserved family tree), could be traced back to Ali, the Prophet's son-in-law and cousin. Khaled didn't miss a single one of the five daily prayers and, as if that were not enough, he prayed all the time—standing, sitting, or lying down. He was known in the neighborhood as "the mullah" as a sign of respect. Meanwhile Rami called him *al shabah*, the ghost.

On the ensuing mornings, a tired, shivering Rami would join Tarek at the crossroads with Street 40, the main route that led to the local market, with a metal tray balanced on his head, ready to walk the alleyways of a still-sleeping Fallujah. This was how Rami learned the strain of getting up early, but also that the dawn was worth it. You had to suffer to witness the innocence of the five o'clock light, to see the first traders opening their eyes as they opened their stalls, catch the sweet smell of bread wafting from ovens, and watch men sipping black cardamom tea. These rare moments of respite were jewels of happiness.

Samiya judiciously left Ahmed a few crumbs of authority. It was decided that Rami and Tarek would give their takings to their father. He would often be sitting at the counter of his makeshift little business adjoining the house, and he took this role very seriously.

When his sons arrived home, Ahmed would always congratulate one and harangue the other.

"What do mean, you haven't sold any? How does Tarek manage it? How are you going to succeed in life?"

That last question was one Rami would ask himself until the end of his days.

Samiya constantly lurked in the shadows, waiting to catch Rami out. And with her was Saad, her eldest, her accomplice, always ready to obey her orders. Saad was the unruliest of Samiya's children. More assertive than the others, cleverer, the leader of the three brothers. He was very like his mother and used the same authoritarian tone with his younger brothers. He didn't speak, he issued orders. Ayad here, Riyad over there, fetch this, put that there. He leapt at any opportunity to instill his law. Or his mother's.

Ahmed, who was overwhelmed by life—and by death—often forgot his coat when he went out to run his shop. His long raincoat, in which he always kept some change, would stay there on a wooden chair, like bait at the mercy of predators. Saad regularly made the most of his stepfather's oversight to rifle through the pockets. With Rami watching, Saad would shamelessly take a few dinars and slip them into his own pocket. This happened several times, but Rami never spoke out. He never mentioned it to Samiya, whom he didn't trust at all. Silent injustice was far better than a thunderbolt.

"Are you with me or not?" Tarek asked one March morning when Rami was daydreaming.

"I'm with you."

"How many have you sold?"

"None, I don't have your blue eyes," Rami joked, with the repartee he'd learned from Hatem, who had a gift for irritating his older brother.

Tarek froze and scowled.

"The old woman will give you hell again if you don't sell any. And do you like always having little Saad sniggering next to her?"

Rami didn't answer. Tarek wouldn't understand. Whatever he did, Samiya always found some excuse to have a go at him. He was nothing, she'd reminded him of that. Anyway, trade wasn't his strong point. He always went home empty-handed.

When Rami and Tarek went into their father's shop, Samiya came in behind them with a coat over her arm. She glowered at Rami before handing the coat to her husband and whispering something in his ear.

Ahmed's face changed color.

"Did you touch my coat, Rami?"

Caught unawares, the child didn't know what to say. Saad must have been at it again, but how could he explain? It was too late, no one would believe a word he said. Confronted by his father and feeling as if he'd been ambushed, Rami was incapable of reacting. He flushed till his ears burned. In his father's eyes he was guilty.

"A thief! My son's a thief!"

Rami would never forget what happened next.

Ahmed leapt off his chair and Rami instantly protected his head—this wasn't the first time he'd been subjected to his father's fury. But on this particular day Ahmed beat him so hard he seemed to want to destroy him. The slaps became punches and then kicks. Rami's body cowered. Ahmed tried to pull aside Rami's arms that were crossed over his face as he lay in the fetal position. And when he couldn't get to the boy with his feet, he thrashed him with his belt.

"Get up!" Ahmed yelled.

His eyes were bulging from their sockets. Rami stood up and, in a moment of courage or madness, faced up to his father. Shaking in pain and fighting back tears, he stood tall in the face of injustice and lies. Tarek was left speechless, unable to protest or to protect his brother. And all the while Saad smiled. A final slap knocked Rami to the floor, breaking the last thread that bound him to his father. His left eardrum sent pain drilling into his head.

From that day forward, Rami was deaf in one ear.

THE SLAP, THE FORECOURT, AND STOP CLUNY

(Summer 1988)

ONE MEMORY was an especially searing pain in the middle of a boring summer, on a sunny day when the hourglass had no sand and the stifling heat slowed the passage of time. The previous day my father had asked me to take delivery of a package of postcards, hand over the money that he'd left on top of the window, and be sure to say *good afternoon* and *thank you* to the man. It was very important, he said that several times, without explaining whether the important thing was saying *good afternoon* or being sure to take the parcel. He was expecting his monthly delivery of accordion postcards, the ones he sold on the forecourt of Notre-Dame and that tourists so enjoyed unfolding.

By getting his supplies from a wholesaler, he paid 1.50 apiece for these concertinas of postcards. He then sold them to tourists for a nice round ten francs. There were two advantages to a ten-franc coin: no need to make change and less risk of being caught red-handed by the police. Plus his customers were getting the cards for less than they would pay in souvenir shops. It was a win-win situation. My father had just run out of stock, which was why the delivery was so vital.

I'd asked a group of friends over that afternoon. After we'd spent hours on the game console, my exasperated mother sent us outside to play. She didn't want a gang of zombies in the house while she went out to do her shopping.

We were delighted and played an improvised soccer match in the neighborhood. Engrossed in the game, the step overs, tunnels, and undeclared fouls, I forgot about the delivery man. I didn't have a watch. When I did remember, it was too late. At the end of the day, I asked two of my friends to come home with me, convinced my father wouldn't lose his temper if they were there. I was wrong.

He was waiting for me, looking furious.

I stood there in front of him, petrified, not knowing what to say.

"What happened to my delivery?"

The room was still scorching from the summer sun and the tension cranked up a notch, like during a duel in a dark, violent Western. A duel between a father and his son. I was the gangster and he the sheriff. I had done wrong and would have to pay. Bodies motionless, eyes locked. An imagined wind blew through the overheated living room. Beside us, my friends were caught in the cross fire of a conflict, and hoped for just one thing: a happy outcome. All that was missing were the pistols and the holsters.

Then my father brought the duel to an end. I didn't see it coming. I felt the pain even before I understood. The slap was dealt, reverberating around the room. It knocked the breath out of me. My father's left hand propelled me into the stars. The duel was lost, the show over, the curtain came down. My head was spinning. I had cramps in my stomach and daggers in my heart. That slap made far more noise than the few words my father occasionally spat out. To avoid crying in front of my friends, I let out a peal of laughter. A nasty, almost demonic laugh. I lost all sensation in my body. The world seemed rinsed of color. Most likely the rage of humiliation; definitely an intense stress mingled with euphoria. I just couldn't stop laughing and this seemed to throw my father. My mother started yelling at him.

"Why?" she screamed. "Look what you did!"

I heard my friend Kader whistle behind me. I didn't dare turn around. I didn't want to see anyone.

"Shit, what a slap! You really went for it, mister, I gotta say! And, Rami, you're laughing? You're nuts."

Kader's voice brought me back to my senses. As did my father's, asking them to please go home. I saw my friends to the door. When it slammed shut, I collapsed into my mother's arms. My father went back to whatever he'd been doing. The crackle of the TV news. A sound of plates. I was in shock. I could still feel his hand. My father had never hit me before. It was once I'd experienced it physically, on my own cheek, that I started to think about violence. Was it warranted? I was confused by the injustice of it.

I didn't understand this violence, but I hated it.

That evening the telephone rang. I'd gone to bed early and my father came to sit on the edge of my bed after taking the call.

"Can I tell you?"

He told me. The delivery man hadn't come. There'd been some logistical problem, two addresses had been mixed up. So, yes, I'd forgotten my responsibility, but I hadn't been entirely to blame. I hadn't deserved that slap.

"Will you forgive me, mine son?"

I nodded.

"Good night, mine son."

"It's *my* son, Dad."

He looked at me one last time and smiled, before getting up and turning out the light.

"Good night, my son."

For several seconds I watched the shadows cast on the ceiling by a huge freight train. Then, lying in the darkness, I started imagining their phone conversation, or perhaps it was a dream.

Hello, Mr. Ahmed... I'm so sorry, our deliveryman got all mixed up... a mistake with the address... Yes, the deliveryman will be there tomorrow without fail... Yes, it's totally our fault. Your son's fault? No, this has nothing to do with your boy. Is he innocent? Of course, absolutely innocent. I do hope you didn't make him pay for our mistake, Mr. Ahmed.

That wouldn't be fair, you know. And injustice breeds anger. And anger breeds violence. And God alone knows what violence leads to, Mr. Ahmed. No, the mistake won't happen again, Mr. Ahmed. I hope so for you too. I have my eye on you, Mr. Ahmed.

I fell asleep with the image of my father's face full of remorse. He never raised a hand to me again.

———

As far back as I can remember, three closely linked feelings were part of my life: differentness, lies, and loneliness. These early companions forged the person I've become.

Differentness. We weren't far off, just on the threshold of other people's normality. Hardly anything could have been more disconcerting than that in-between state. Being on the margin of what was normal. Neither too close nor too far removed. On the fringes. What I wanted more than anything was to melt into the crowd. I wanted a name like other boys, Karim or François, I didn't really care, I'd had enough of being asked, "Euph...what? Euphrates? That's unusual, where's that from?"

What to say? That my name was from a faraway place I didn't know? That we were a minority within a minority? Most of the families on our street were immigrants from North Africa or Portugal. We were the only people from farther afield. When I was asked about my family history, I told people the one fact I knew: I was from Iraq. Kader, who was from Morocco, had already asked me all about it.

"Iraq? What's Iraq? Is that an Arab place? Couldn't you be Moroccan or Algerian like everyone else? That's too weird, you're just not normal."

I was deeply hurt by his comment. This Iraq was a beautiful far-off country and it really did exist, my father had promised me. People there spoke Arabic, a different version, granted, but still Arabic. How could I describe it when I didn't know it?

When my father was in a good mood he would answer that question.

"So, take France as an example. It's known for its baguettes and cheeses. There are more than five hundred types of cheese. That's one way of describing France. Well, Iraq's the same but with dates. We have more than five hundred varieties of dates. That's what Iraq is," he concluded with the ironic tone he used on good days.

"In fact," he added after a pause, "there's one very rare variety of date that only grows every ten years. It's a dark blue color. It won't grow unless it's on its own, away from yellow dates, which makes it almost impossible to cultivate. You can tell people that too."

A blue date? I didn't know whether I was supposed to take this seriously, and anyway, I couldn't see myself telling Kader about it, he was bound to make fun of me.

I would learn to love dates much later, and I would keep this enigmatic detail of my father's for anyone who deigned to ask me the recurring question. For a long while it became my quirky answer to everyone who asked about my roots.

No one around me looked like me. I had a few native-born French friends, but mostly they were Malian, Algerian, or Moroccan like Kader. Each of them carried his satchel and his culture on his back. Their story was that they came from former French colonies, their parents had been brought here by force to work in mines or on building sites, and they'd stayed. People said that the children carried their forebears' suffering within them. Did I carry my forebears' suffering? And who exactly were they? I was and still am the custodian of a history that has no colonial past with France.

To my parents, France was an asylum, a refuge. It didn't matter that I'd arrived in this world in France and with its language, I felt imprisoned in a different family history. I probably wasn't normal here and didn't belong, as Kader implied. The truth is I've never really known what that means. This shifting, unclassifiable identity has been a silent and burdensome partner my whole life. I wanted to model myself on the others, exercise an identity transfer.

One day when I was walking along the street with the dancing poplars, I caught up with my father on his way home from work. We walked the rest of the way together and I asked him about this.

"Dad, what does being normal mean?"

"Do you feel normal?"

"Nope."

"Is it bad not being like other people?"

"I dunno, but *I* want to be like other people."

"Anything but that, my son, anything but that. Don't be like other people. Don't settle for what people tell you to be. Try to do things you can't yet do. Try to go where you're not expected to go. Being normal doesn't mean wanting to be like other people. It means only doing what you can already do. And not taking any risks. What matters is to be yourself. I work hard so that you can be you. You'll understand one day."

"Okay. And, Dad?"

"Yes?"

"Is the story about the blue dates true?"

"Do you like the story?"

"If it's true, yes."

"It's up to you to decide if it's true."

———

The following Saturday I decided to be proactive.

A long metallic squeal bored into my eardrums. The dying scream of a Métro train being degassed made me think of a horse snorting impatiently, raring to keep galloping. I looked up at the map just under the emergency lever and searched for the yellow line, the narrow one that represented Line 1. I needed to change trains. I found it as the buzzing sound warned that the doors were closing and leapt off the carriage just in time. Porte Maillot station. My connection point where no one exchanged a word. I walked along a corridor papered with smiling ads about the joys of life and contradicted by cohorts of stooped, withdrawn passengers who passed without looking at one another like a uniform mass of individuals only just missing collisions in an automated dance.

A smell of sulfur mixed with engine oil nagged at my nostrils and hung over this human tide. I turned to the right and weaved my way through to escape the smell, but it stayed with me all the way down the stairs, on the rubber guardrail, and onto the station platform. The next line was also yellow, but slightly thicker. It was the RER C line to Saint-Michel. I started to feel excited when the doors to the red, white, and blue train snapped shut and a woman's voice on the public-address system announced the next station with peculiar joy.

Notre-Dame. Notre-Dame. I couldn't shake off the smell of sulfur until I reached fresh air at the exit. It stalked me like a silent, hunched shadow.

It was drizzling outside. On the slippery paving stones of the forecourt, I met Robert and Zezette, Jewish Tunisian brothers who also sold postcards and whom my father really liked. They were his favorite fellow salesmen. Over-the-top characters who bickered all day, sometimes even coming to blows, even though they couldn't live without each other. When they saw me, they hugged me and fought to be the first to slip a fifty-franc note into my pocket. Farther on, I shook hands with Ali, also a postcard seller, a rather introverted Algerian who answered every question with a drowsy *tyyyypical*. My father was nowhere to be seen. Not on the bench where he usually stopped for a snack nor in Rosa's, the regulars' brasserie.

"Isn't he here?" I asked Ali.

"No, sonny, they took him this morning, tyyyypical."

They—the local plainclothes police officers—knew everyone in the gang by their first names. And the gang knew them equally well. They had to take someone in for questioning every now and then for the record at their precinct, so everyone played cat and mouse with one group trying to catch the other, which tried to escape. That day was my father's turn. With my heart pounding, I imagined them saying, "Come on, Rami, it's your day. Let's go." My father wasn't doing anything wrong: Like Ali and the others, he sold postcards to tourists. The square in front of Notre-Dame was one of the most visited sites in the world. My father's work wasn't easy: He had to walk up and down those paving stones under a blazing sun or, by contrast, the damp and implacable cold of Parisian winters. And do it discreetly but be prepared to be taken in for questioning by the police.

These unlicensed hawkers were usually released after a few hours. Their cards of the Eiffel Tower, Notre-Dame, and Sacré-Cœur were confiscated, they were asked to sign a statement and then to sit in a cell.

"Go wait for him at the Cluny," Ali suggested. "I'll tell him you came by."

"Thanks, Ali."

"No problem."

The Stop Cluny was my father's favorite café. Its comforting smell of damp cigarettes and warm croissants and my father's conversations with his Iraqi friends—which always went on too long—were a part of my childhood. The group of them didn't waste any time soaking up the sun, they stayed inside. The Stop Cluny was a small oasis for sometimes heated debate, and, sitting sipping my apricot juice, I was an honored spectator.

About an hour went by before I spotted him in the distance with his leather bag over his shoulder. Almost before he'd opened the door, he ordered an apricot juice and a strong espresso before giving me a kiss.

"Hi, mine son. Ali said you came over."

"On my own," I replied, delighted with myself.

He nodded and sat down, not giving any explanation for his absence, and took out a packet of cigarettes. He smelled of eau de cologne and sweat. He smoked in silence and watched me with his usual faraway look. I detected some pride in his expression, but also concern. Had he guessed why I was there? Perhaps the time had come to shed some light on whatever it was that was too complicated? A father-son thing. The previous week he'd put up barriers. But today, in that oasis nowhere near home, would they come tumbling down?

"Mine son, I'm going to tell you something. I can't talk." He paused before continuing. "I have to whisper. Iraq isn't just a country, mine son. Iraq is a society of whispers. It's a place where you can't survive without lying. And I've never liked lying."

I couldn't see where he was going with this.

"What about the photo? And the card?"

My father sat in silence, staring at some point in the distance, far from the café, as if regretting he'd said too much. Or perhaps it was too painful. Glumness was his chief personality trait. I couldn't remember a single light-hearted conversation with him. Everything was political. Everything was serious. Was he trying to create a diversion? To avoid saying anything yet again? I sat upright in my chair, firm and determined, with my elbows on the table, and I waited patiently for him to start whispering. I was ready to produce the card with the false name that I'd found in the suitcase. I wanted my father to tell me his story, to confide in me about his past at last. He looked around several times as if he thought he was being watched. I was surprised to detect a sort of feverishness I hadn't seen in him before. His mouth opened slightly—perhaps to expel a sigh at an unnecessarily cruel world—then closed again onto his wretched cigarette. He took a deep breath like someone about to make a big speech, then heaved another sigh. A sigh of resignation. I desperately hoped that the words would eventually come out one after the other to reveal this world that I so wanted to understand. They never came.

For the first time I grasped that this excruciating difficulty with talking comprised several different strata and the first of these was silence. Over the years I came to terms with it. So much so that I came to visualize it as a cloud of ash and reticence. On that day, though, as I sat facing my father, I didn't say another word.

What was the point? It was too soon. Or too late. I gave up on the interrogative pronouns and drew a veil over my questions. Realizing I was upset, he took out a notebook and pen and started writing. Dozens of names. Then he tore out the page and gave it to me.

"You have a huge family," he said. "It's here on this piece of paper and over there in Iraq."

At least I hadn't come for nothing. How I looked at that list, reading it, dreaming about it, projecting it onto walls and faces and my fantasies of the distant homeland. On the sheet of paper was a list of first names: Riad, Ayad, Taghrid…And one name at the top of the page: Fallujah. My father had circled it and written, *your hometown*.

I gauged the element of chance in life's journey: I was born in Paris but should have been born in Fallujah, a place I'd never set foot in, and my name should have been on that list. No one chooses where they are born. Life always starts with this injustice. Did we really have any choice? From that moment on I was dogged by a strange feeling; I couldn't say whether it was guilt for being lucky or regret for an unknown life that, in the normal course of events, would have been my destiny. My father claimed that all these people knew my name and had even seen photos of my sister and me, while we knew nothing of them. He did at least give me this: knowing that I was a tiny part of a huge family. And the strength and confidence to grant myself this affiliation fueled my questions. I too had a family, and nothing and no one could take that from me.

Of course, the war meant we couldn't meet, but time would do its work. My father and I took the Métro home together. He didn't utter a word on the train, but stayed silent for the whole journey, his usual self, and the smell of sulfur nagged at my nostrils again.

The following Saturday was the beginning of the summer vacation. All through my childhood the last day of school was always the hardest. It heralded everyone else's departure and the beginning of boredom and loneliness. That summer some of my friends were off to join cousins by the sea, others going to visit their grandparents in the country. But we had nowhere to go. This distant Iraq was still a mystery to my sister and myself. I thought about it all the time. Arwa was growing up and she too started voicing questions—the same ones that I did—that went unanswered. At least I had that list. I shared it with Arwa, and we never tired of reading it and imagining our family.

But that wasn't enough; and I still felt alone in the world. I didn't have sufficient points of reference and my father worried about this, but clearly didn't know how to remedy it.

Over the coming weeks, fate fulfilled my expectations with two telephone calls that changed my life.

The first was from our family in Iraq. I could hear cries of joy coming from the handset, as well as my mother's laughter and crying, my father's solemn voice. Then the apartment fell silent again. Not with the weighty silence I'd known since I was little, nor the sinister shadow of a dictator that hung over Stop Cluny. More a silence filled with inquiring glances. Something was about to happen. My father was smoking more than usual, my mother snapped at the smallest things, and the two of them sometimes talked far too loudly and sometimes far too quietly. During these conversations, I was strictly forbidden to ask any questions. They were discussing important matters, grown-up things. One evening I overheard them talking again, there was murmuring coming from their bedroom. I pressed my ear to their door, trying to catch a few words that buzzed and then melted before reaching my ears. Still, I did manage to make out some snatches of conversation.

"Live there? Are you crazy? And do what? Wafa, this isn't peace. There'll never be peace with him. You'll see."

"But at least we'd have a big house. We'd have a family."

"What family? Yours? The family that's watching me from heaven? I don't have anyone left there, I have no family left. Iraq is finished. So long as he's there, there's no future. And you always dreamed of Paris, well, you're here now. Do you realize how lucky you are?"

"Lucky? We have nothing, no house, no stability, no family!"

"What are you talking about? We have peace here! And that's a real luxury. Peace!"

"I'll never cope like this. I miss my family, I want to see them."

"Go see them! I don't care! You're such a pain!"

A slam of the wardrobe door. Sobbing, footsteps, curses directed at the sky. Then silence. I went back to my bedroom and couldn't get to sleep until well into the night.

———

The next day my parents weren't talking to each other. The tension was palpable, hanging in the air. I wished I could scoop it up and throw it out the window. That evening my father kept to himself, deep in thought. As I watched the scrolls of smoke coming from his nose, I noticed that the way he looked at me had changed.

It wasn't long before the second phone call was made. And it was more discreet: My father had clearly taken the phone all the way to the kitchen and dialed the number himself. Again, I pressed my ear to the door. He was speaking in Arabic and I know only a few words. Journey, plane, return ticket, passport, Baghdad, list. His voice was full of misgivings. When he hung up, I could tell he'd reached a decision. The war was abating, peace opening its arms to us, there was my loneliness and his fight with my mother— he may well have been thinking this truce presented an opportunity. He opened the door and looked at me.

"Come sit down with me," he said, putting an arm around my shoulders. "You're finally going to see your family."

"The one that knows us?"

"The one that knows you."

"Are we going to go live there?"

He looked me right in the eye. "We're not going to live there. You and your sister will go with your mother and then you'll come back to France."

"You're not coming?"

"I can't come. Did you keep the list?"

I took it from my pocket.

"I'd rather you didn't take it with you."

"Why not?"

"Lists of names are never a good idea over there. I'll explain one day but do as you're told."

I didn't understand this request, nor why he wasn't coming with us. I promised I would throw the list away once I'd learned all the names by heart, so it could be a part of me before we set off. I was determined to do the exact opposite—to slip it in my pocket and hide it. I needed that list to find myself. How else would I manage with this huge family?

Then he explained briefly that it was risky sending my mother, my sister, and me over there, but it was possible without him. He also featured on a list of names—I didn't grasp why. But he'd checked and we had nothing to fear, he'd called a friend who knew his brothers, who were soldiers and whom he hadn't seen since he left Iraq.

"So I have even more uncles, then?"

He smiled at me. "Like I said, your family's huge."

My father had never mentioned his brothers to me. I remembered what he'd said during the fight with my mother: *I don't have anyone left there. Iraq is finished.*

Well, for me Iraq was about to start. My vacation was finally taking shape, a slightly unusual vacation but there would definitely be plenty of stories to tell my friends. I was convinced that, by making one phone call, my father had found the answer to my loneliness. Iraq, which had always seemed a distant entity comprising photos and cousins on the phone, was going to materialize at last. I was going to see my parents' country and this huge family I didn't know.

THE TRIP

(Summer 1989)

MY MOTHER, my sister, and I boarded an Iraqi Airways flight to Baghdad. A five-hour overnight flight toward the unknown. I didn't sleep at all, euphoric at the idea of putting faces to the names on the list in my pocket. As we disembarked from the plane and were scorched by the hot wind that flattened our hair to our heads, I was inwardly clutching my mother's skirt. I steadied myself with thoughts of dromedaries and the vast country that had been home to my two Middle Eastern escapees.

In Baghdad's international airport terminal, apathetic mustached men checked our passports. Just one pane of glass lay between customs and the endgame. My family was waiting for us on the other side. There were so many of them I couldn't count them. I was wearing a gray suit and a blue tie, and my mouth felt furry. After the last checkpoint, the door opened onto an exuberant crowd chanting our names. An Arabic welcome. Euphrates, Arwa, Wafa! They all had their arms raised and opened wide. I moved from one cheek to the next, not really knowing what was happening. We were hugged and cheered and smothered with kisses. Then we just sat together for a while. The whole experience took my breath away. There they all were in the flesh. As we headed for the exit, I noticed three men in military uniform walking a little apart from my jubilant family.

"They're your uncles from Fallujah," my mother explained. "Riyad, Ayad, and Saad."

The three of them waved at me. They seemed very different from my mother's family. I nodded in reply and two of them smiled at me. Then they left as mysteriously as they'd appeared, but I didn't know why.

"Don't worry, you'll see them soon," my mother whispered in my ear. "You'll go visit them in Fallujah."

We formed a convoy of about twenty cars and I was struck by how modern this country I'd daydreamed about was. Where were the sand dunes and camels? The airport, asphalt roads, American cars, metal streetlights illuminating the date palms; it was nothing like I'd imagined. Oldsmobiles, Cadillacs, and Pontiacs—cars I'd only seen on TV in series like *Starsky and Hutch*. Coming to Iraq allowed me to establish a fact: "Mom, we're poor in France!"

"Well, what did you think?"

I didn't think anything because I didn't know anything. In France we didn't have a car and lived in a small apartment, but here huge cars straight out of Hollywood movies were parked outside enormous houses.

Along the way I noticed giant portraits of a man, some-times in military uniform, sometimes in a white suit and black hat. He looked powerful and glorious but there was also something strangely, almost mysteriously serene about him. He must have been the man whose name we weren't allowed to say; my father had warned me about this before the trip.

"The Iraq you're visiting is a dictatorship," he'd said.

"What's a dictatorship?"

"It's a country where everyone whispers. You and your sister mustn't talk too loudly, no one speaks out loud, un-less it about something unimportant. You understand?"

"I dunno."

"You mustn't comment on what you see. In the land of whispers, you too must whisper."

Seeing that succession of giant portraits, I felt I was being watched by this man who radiated a sort of fear-inducing conviction. Of course, the fear was irrational be-cause these were only pictures, but I came to realize that everyone shared this fear. Our happiness was short-lived, dampened by my cousin Taghrid's warning: She said we must never say Saddam Hussein's name out on the street. With all the imagination of a six-year-old, Arwa heard the thing she wasn't allowed to do and decided to go right ahead and do it.

"Saddam!" she squealed, raising her arms defiantly.

Every face on the street turned to look at us. A man dressed in black and wearing a hat got up from a bench not far away and stared at us. Time stood still. The pandemonium of traffic became just muted background noise. Taghrid gave him a wave to try to defuse the situation. The man, whose face we could barely make out, didn't respond. He kept watching us for a while and then walked away. Lowered eyes, slow movements, forced smiles. No one in the family complained or raised the subject. Even fear was pretending. Furious as well as distraught, Taghrid rushed over and shut us in the car. We left the neighborhood immediately and headed for Aunt Sumaya's house. Taghrid yelled as we drove along. Arwa and I were baffled, and we sat in silence, trying to understand what had just happened. Who was that man? Then I remembered my father's advice. Perhaps that was what a dictatorship was: The reason for unspoken words at home, silencing the name of the man my father had fled. The reason for whispering.

———

A week after we arrived in Baghdad, my three uncles came to collect me to go to Fallujah, Rami's hometown. We didn't talk much on the way there. I still wasn't doing very well in Arabic, catching only every other word, so I concentrated on their expressions. They stared at me, fascinated by this son of a brother they hadn't seen for sixteen years. And who'd left Iraq with no warning. They claimed they'd received only one handwritten letter, eight years after their brother left, announcing my birth. It described a new life in France, promised to give news from time to time, and asked them not to worry about him. Then the Iran-Iraq War had started, and another eight years had gone by with no news.

After the truce and the all-important phone call, here I was with them on the way to Rami's childhood, and I still didn't really know who Rami was.

SAAD

(Fall 1953)

RAMI WAS now forbidden to dream about his dead mother, there must be no sign of her anywhere, not in his words nor his tears nor his night terrors. Samiya gave him no respite. She circled her prey, strangled it, stopped it from making any progress. She came to give him the instruction one night: Rami woke and was terrified by the expressionless eyes peering at him. His blood pounded in his temples, his heart thudded in his ears.

"You must stop calling for her, d'you understand?" Samiya reprimanded him. "She's gone, she's dead."

Rami nodded. He mustn't annoy Samiya. He wouldn't mention Muhja again. His mother's name would fall into a bottomless well, but no one could stop him from thinking about her in secret. Whatever the nights were like, whatever the days, he would never wipe her from his memory, Muhja would be his psychological diamond. It would be his remedy for this absence, and Samiya would never know. How else could he survive? In order to withstand the trials

of his day-to-day life as a motherless child, Rami now had
to set aside his emotions. To keep his head above water he
learned to surround himself with a steep stealthy barrier
against suffering. He'd become a child of the green bridge.
A certified diver who could now swim in the tumultuous
waters of the Euphrates. Rami had overcome death, he
would survive Samiya. From now on he would be just a
silent shadow through all the stunts laid on by this other
woman and Saad, *her* son, her helper, her accomplice.

On a pale morning during the *asifa*, when one identi-
cal day followed another, three faces had been staring at
the ground for about ten minutes. Saad and his brothers
in the shade of the garden's only date palm. Their three
hunched bodies formed a semicircle, improvising a bizarre
ceremony as they searched for a scrap of skin. Riyad and
Ayad, on the orders of their young leader Saad, scoured
every tiny tuft of grass, every last detail of the tiled path
that led to the henhouse. Nothing was left to chance.

"We have to find it and stick it back on my finger. Find
it or I'm going to die, I'm warning you," Saad insisted, giving up and crouching against a low wall, clasping his left
index finger with his right hand. He was upset, terrorized
to think his finger might never be the same, his finger
which was so useful for catching lizards and other small
creatures.

He had a preference for winged insects, dangerous
venomous ones. Flies were just harmless prey. He was after
zeneburs, orange-colored Asian hornets that everyone was
afraid of and whose sting could sometimes kill children

and the elderly. They also caused significant damage to the surrounding fields and they besieged beehives, decimating the bee population. Saad lured them with sugar on the paving stones of the small patio. Once the trap was set, he imprisoned them in an overturned glass, and this led to a fatal state of lethargy, which thrilled him. He took malicious delight in slowly asphyxiating them. His fascination was mingled with excitement, not about death itself but the means of achieving it: suffering and fear. With a particular predilection for the point when he could cut it short or prolong it. It depended on his mood. Sometimes he tortured them. Using his English army penknife, which his mother had stolen from British soldiers, he picked them apart, cutting off the legs, wings, and stinger. Then he waited for the critical moment, the penultimate breath, before separating the head from the body. Finally, he hunkered down, like a satisfied executioner, to study the hornet's death throes through a magnifying glass. Alone with this silent death. Saad had serious problems, Rami could see that clearly.

On other occasions, though these were much rarer, he would release his victims, almost certainly to revel in his total power on the question of life or death, his power over such an insignificant creature.

Saad was not yet ten years old.

Fifteen minutes before the search in the garden, he'd been trying to impress his brothers by climbing to the top of the palm tree's rough trunk. As he came back down, one hand had lost its grip and he'd clung to a sharp hunk of bark. When he saw a small scrap of skin that had been torn off, he started screaming, panicking that a part of his anatomy would be lost forever. He might have enjoyed torturing insects but was an excessive hypochondriac when it came to his own body.

"That piece of skin is incredibly precious, we have to find it!" he'd roared.

"Don't worry, your skin'll grow back!" Riyad had replied.

Despite his younger brother's incredulity, Saad had insisted: "This is a matter of life and death. Find it or I'll kill myself."

Saad had a similar personality to Samiya's and used the same melodramatic tone of voice to instill his law. He could be very persuasive in the heat of his over-the-top behavior and need to dominate—Rami had learned this the hard way.

Rami was hiding behind a garden wall, watching the scene. He wondered why Saad had always been so fascinated by death. The boy used anything as a pretext for suicide, particularly if he was refused something he wanted. And this attitude no longer surprised anyone. They'd all grown used to fits of anger from the "little dictator." Rami had never rebuked Saad for the ambush set by Samiya that had cost him an eardrum. After the alleged theft, not once had Rami tried to plead his own case with his father. When he thought about it, he wondered whether Saad too was the victim of a chaotic life—his father had died suddenly. At least they had the loss of a cornerstone in common. Rami understood. He knew. He'd been there.

Even so, Rami attached more importance to how Samiya's tyranny affected her son. What would happen if Saad had nothing else to refer to but his mother's behavior? There was a danger that implicit permission to cause suffering to others would be imprinted on him forever. It was a safe bet that, left to his own devices, Saad would soon tire of torturing insects and be irrevocably drawn to more dangerous options. Young torturers learned cruelty by identifying with the adults around them. Rami was sure that no one was born cruel or a killer.

And so he had forgiven Saad and, without telling him as much, did his best to understand him. Saad was still a child, perhaps it wasn't too late. How else to explain his reaction to losing a tiny scrap of skin? There must have been some innocence left in his depths. Rami pitied his stepbrother and could see the hold Samiya had over him. The boy needed to be released from his mother's clutches. And to achieve that, Rami had to find Saad's Achilles' heel. Always lost in his own thoughts and his sense of foreboding, he'd never guessed that Saad's weakness was right there in front of him.

"I got it! I got it!" cried Riyad, brandishing a fragment of graying skin.

"Quick, give it back!" howled Saad, who then rushed inside to find a length of fabric to help bring the skin back to life.

Rami smiled. It had just clicked. There was the chink in the armor: in his fear of death, a fear so strong it was obsessive. He went off to find Saad.

"You need a tomato and some salt."

"What?" Saad asked, amazed.

"You have to cut a tomato in two, sprinkle it with salt, and put it on the cut," Rami explained, putting a hand on Saad's shoulder. "That's what we do when we have a wound, it disinfects it. It's what all great men of the desert do."

Unaccustomed to conversations with Rami, Saad looked disconcerted.

"What would you know?" he asked tartly. He was being wary. Much as he enjoyed being taken seriously, he must still keep his distance from *the other boy*, as his mother had told him to. He watched Rami and listened to him as he wound the fabric around his swollen finger.

"I know because I was once stung by a black scorpion."

Rami understood Saad's tune. In the sheet music of coercion, you always had to play a higher note than him.

"A *zenebur* sting is very painful," Saad retorted, unblinking. Then he slowly moved closer to Rami as curiosity gradually overtook suspicion. Rami was luring Saad to just where he wanted him. He'd opened the chink, now he had to choose the right words. He may not have used words often, but he could occasionally wield them with precision. Saad remembered what his mother had said to Rami: *You're nothing*. But *the other boy* wasn't nothing, he'd taken on a black scorpion. While he, the reputedly tough little dictator, had only had dealings with a garden-variety orange hornet.

"Show me."

Rami raised his eyebrows. "Don't you believe me?"

"Show me the black scorpion bite."

Rami pulled up his pants to show his left ankle. There was a line of small, raised red spots. A scar Rami was always proud to explain.

"I was leaning against a wall with my eyes closed. I was playing with Hatem. When I turned around, I saw the black scorpion circling my feet. I tried to stamp on it and it bit me with its venomous tail. I screamed like I'd never screamed before."

"Is that story true?" Saad asked skeptically.

"Do you like it?"

"If it's true, yes."

"Then it's true."

Saad stood openmouthed. Rami was telling the truth.

"And what happened after that?" asked Saad, obviously won over.

"After that I could feel the venom going up to my calf, then my knee. My right leg started to feel numb. If it wasn't for the salted tomato on my ankle to draw out the venom, I'd have died."

"Died?"

"Yes, died. Black scorpions are lethal, didn't you know that?"

Rami looked him right in the eye. The little dictator resorted to just a shake of the head to mean: No, I didn't know that. Rami was gradually winning his respect. Alone, away from Samiya, and therefore vulnerable, Saad was just a credulous child who—in turn—had walked right into an ambush.

"This has to stay between the two of us, okay? You can't tell this to just anyone. No one, in fact. Also I wanted to say, I don't hold the thing with my dad's coat against you. It wasn't your fault. Now go find a tomato and some salt, and do what I tell you, that's a brother's advice."

"A brother?"

"A brother."

Wary, still putting on a brave face, Saad tried to identify the wrong note in what Rami was saying. He would never admit it but all he could think about was putting a salted tomato on his wound. For the first time Saad was forced to lay down his weapons. He turned on his heel without another word and went off to the kitchen.

And Rami smiled to himself.

SAAD

(Summer 1989)

WHEN WE reached my uncles' home, I noticed how different the scenery was. If Baghdad was a modern city, Fallujah felt like being in the countryside, beautiful countryside. Was this the Ardèche vacation I'd dreamed of? My weekend in Normandy? We were a long way from France, but I finally understood what "visiting family" meant. The house was just as I'd imagined, childishly simple. A rectangular block surrounded by a garden. A chicken coop. And a very old, twice-widowed lady dressed in black standing on the front doorstep. Samiya, Rami's formidable stepmother.

She introduced herself as my grandmother, so I was to call her Bibi. She pinched my cheeks, gave me a sloppy kiss, and took my hand. I struggled in vain to disguise my aversion to her smell, the way she looked at me, and her forced smile. A grandmother? I'd never had one. I didn't have the user's manual. I noticed that Samiya and my uncles all had a gap between their front teeth, and I was fascinated by the physical similarity. I was also surprised that I found it easier to understand what they were saying. People here seemed to speak more slowly than in Baghdad, which made their dialect clearer and more soothing. Uncle Saad seemed distant compared to the others, almost distrustful. But he still offered to give me a long tour of the Euphrates. Had he sensed my discomfort?

"I'll show you the river you're named after," he said.

We set off at about two in the afternoon with the sun at its zenith. The AC in the car, a white Volkswagen, no longer worked and the open windows let in heat blasting like a hair dryer. Uncle Saad was friendlier without the others. He started talking about anything and everything, describing his hometown and his Volkswagen Barasili. He claimed it was what soldiers drove. All officers were issued one by the government. Since the war, Fallujah had become a stronghold for generals and other officers loyal to the Baath Party. He did not mention the forbidden name.

"There are two crucially important things here. Pride and reputation."

When we reached the right bank of the Euphrates, it was still just as hot, and the road became a dirt track strewn with stones. Uncle Saad suggested we continue on foot. I was worried about dirtying my new tennis shoes but silenced this concern. *Pride* and *reputation* were important in Fallujah. We made an odd pair.

In Fallujah, just like in Baghdad, you were never alone. There were always people watching you on the street, in cafés and markets, and it was difficult to gauge how well-meaning these watchful eyes were.

The river, which reflected the azure of the sky, was spanned by a green bridge.

"Built by the British," Saad informed me.

As we walked over the bridge to the far bank, I noticed a dozen or so children my age lined up along the edge, holding watermelons and preparing to jump into the water.

"It's traditional," he explained.

I didn't yet know that my father, Rami, had been one of these little divers determinedly braving the current. My head spun at the thought of jumping into the river. I wasn't a very good swimmer and felt incapable of taking on those tempestuous waters that had given me my name.

Once we reached the other side, we sat on a rock and I tried discreetly to clean the soles of my shoes. Saad watched me with a smile, as if this whim of mine didn't surprise him. He wouldn't understand that these Reebok Pumps were a fragment of a legend to me, the greatest NBA players had worn them, the Pump system meant each shoe could adapt perfectly to the foot, and at school people fought to press the basketball-shaped pump on the tongue. Would he have guessed that a new pair was worth nearly a thousand francs? That my father had dug them out at the flea market, completely unaware of their value? Surely not. Maybe telling him about that sort of technology in an old language would be seen as heresy, just as city words and country expressions were sometimes incompatible. When faced with a door that could lead to a total lack of understanding, it's better not to open it.

Uncle Saad sat in almost religious silence as he watched the divers and their crazy, daring acrobatics—the bridge was at least fifteen meters high. The local children seemed to me to be from a different planet. The silence grew longer, and I wondered if my uncle thought I was difficult. After a few minutes I realized that when I turned my head away, I could feel him watching me but when I turned back to him, he looked away. He had lots of nervous tics and he suddenly started rubbing his fingers together, cracking his joints, and swallowing repeatedly. Something was eating him up. I looked around: to my right was a red brick wall, in front of me the river, and to my left the green bridge. Saad was sitting slightly farther back on an invisible line behind my back. His behavior betrayed a jumpiness I couldn't understand. The silence dragged on and I grew increasingly anxious. Everything felt bigger and more dangerous. I'd wound up here alone and vulnerable on the edge of a cliff, battling with dark thoughts that were taking hold of me. What if he pushed me into the water? I felt I'd been trapped, like a fly in a spider's web. A cunningly woven web. I had a sudden urge to flee. After all, I didn't know this Uncle Saad. Then all at once he stood up. I flinched away and also got to my feet, pretending to behave naturally. Saad dusted off his pants and came right up to me. On the slope of that small hillside, he towered over me. He crouched to my level with one arm on his thigh.

"Your father came here a lot. Do you know why?"

I shook my head.

"He didn't like being at home." He stared at me, waiting for a reaction. "Didn't he tell you about any of this?"

"No."

I remembered Stop Cluny and my father's silence.

Saad seemed surprised.

"Just one question," he said.

"Yes?"

"Why didn't he come?"

I didn't know what to say. My father had warned me: *Over there everything is silenced, and no one says anything. It's a land of whispers so it's better to keep quiet.*

Had Saad brought me all this way to talk about taboo subjects? He smiled at my hesitation.

"Tell your father he can come back, tell him black scorpions and *zeneburs* aren't venomous anymore. Tell him those exact words, okay?"

"Okay."

Then he raised an impatient hand and twisted his wrist to check his watch.

"Shall we go?"

Before returning to the road, we crossed back over the bridge and followed the right bank, trying to step on rocks to avoid the mud. Saad also seemed to want to spare his shoes.

We got back into the car, now white-hot from the relentless sun, and we set off again on the road, which was bumpy for several kilometers. The landscape bore witness to the poverty of the surrounding village: Away from the city center there were few paved roads. Occasional fruit stalls alternated with scrap-metal dealers and people selling mutton kebabs. The houses grew fewer and farther between. I counted far more mules than cars. Some carried gas bottles, others carboys of water. I even saw a lone donkey with wheels and a car bumper on its back. People standing on the shoulder waved to us as we passed.

Uncle Saad stopped near a group of men carrying toolboxes. They immediately ran over to our car and surrounded us, elbowing past one another to get to the driver's window as if their lives depended on it. Before lowering the window, Saad explained that the men were out of work and were offering their services: odd jobs, gardening, even unblocking squat toilets with long flexible metal rods. Uncle Saad didn't need anything, but in this sleepy place people took the time to help one another out and chat and just show one another some consideration. Relations between people were very different here than in the city.

After a conversation I didn't fully understand, two men—each with a cigarette in his mouth—climbed into the car with us and sat shyly on the rear seat. They wanted to get to the soccer stadium on Street 40. It was called that because it went to Baghdad, which was only forty miles away from this rural place; these two worlds that usually turned their backs on each other occasionally competed on a soccer pitch.

"That's exactly where we're going," said Saad, looking at them in the rearview mirror.

This didn't sound altogether natural, as if my uncle didn't really know where to go and meeting these two guys was a blessing.

That's how I ended up watching a local soccer match on a near grassless pitch whose white lines had somehow managed to resist the passage of time. Cigarette smoke filled the grandstands that were packed with supercharged men. The Baghdad Air Force Club was taking on the Fallujah Falcons; it was their annual derby. I used this opportunity to study my surroundings; the spectacle around me was far more absorbing than the one on the pitch: fiery scowls, enthusiasm that bordered on hysteria, and appallingly uncomfortable metal seats. The clash looked set to be bitter and tense. I was starting to feel short of breath on the terraces, which were moist and heavy with sweat.

Saad remained impassive amid the electrified crowd. A succession of chants accompanied each acceleration, any missed opportunity, and every oversight from the referee. The bald, uneven pitch became a battlefield between the city and the country. There was nothing friendly about the match now. The stakes lay somewhere altogether different and the stadium had become a theater for social revenge. Fallujah's rural types had to humiliate Baghdad's urbanites. The whole crowd buzzed as it chorused the despair and heartbreak of a town that felt it had been abandoned by the government.

"Fallujah! Fallujah! Strong and proud! Fallujah! Fallujah!"

At that point, child that I was, I hoped desperately for a tie. To soothe all that ardor and save the pride and reputation of this hodgepodge of rage.

An hour and a half later, the ref blew the final whistle and not one goal had been scored. The tension dropped. I was safe and sound. Saad barged through to get us out of the stifling commotion.

On the drive home we stopped at a game room, a place forbidden to women. In a basement, men playing backgammon and dominoes sat around a billiards table which, just like the soccer pitch, was no longer green. Spoons clinked in cups of sugary tea, sending shrill notes through the smoke-filled room, punctuating the rattle of dice on backgammon boards and the smack of dominoes on the table. I instantly liked the darkness and the confidential feel of the place.

Why had Uncle Saad brought me here? Did he want to show me the best parts of Fallujah or the most sinister? What message was he hoping to convey? I felt he'd been trying to say something to me all day; an indefinable mood hung in the air, making me uncomfortable. Luckily, I would soon be back in Baghdad, and then everything would be fine.

On the way to the house I was allowed to hold my uncle's pistol. Unloaded, of course. As I went proudly through the souk toward the family home, I pictured myself as a cowboy with a Colt in his belt, way out in the Wild West.

The market was dusty and noisy but interesting. Exhaust fumes were replaced by animal smells. The perfume of nowhereland, the scent of the back of beyond. Everyone greeted us here, and I learned later that my uncles owed this respect to the Iran-Iraq War. Saad and his brothers had fought and come home as heroes. Riyad had apparently brought down an enemy plane, Saad killed dozens of Iranian soldiers, and Ayad lost half of his left foot because of a shell. They'd even been decorated by the rais himself, the one whose name was only whispered. The photo had been framed and nailed to the living-room wall.

When we arrived back, Bibi Samiya was waiting for us for a late lunch. She instructed her strapping sons to lay out the tablecloth—we would be eating on the ground. She was the boss and exercised an implacable authority despite her advanced years. Everyone obeyed her unquestioningly.

I met my father's eldest brother, Khaled, a mysterious Sufi. He had snow-white hair and blue eyes, a mystical voice and a penetrating gaze; he seemed to live in another world. He spoke little and when he did, it was in a soft voice that heightened his charisma. I grasped that he lived with his sons in a small house somewhere remote, and had made the journey here to meet me. I was struck by his personality which commanded respect, his calm kindly manner which cooled the heated family dynamic. Next to him was my uncle Tarek: very dark-skinned, with a thickset frame and no neck, he was like a blue-eyed Mike Tyson. Everyone watched me during the meal, but only Bibi Samiya spoke. She asked me about my father, his health, and his everyday life. Was he doing well? Would he be coming back? She didn't smile. She stared at me. I got the feeling she was trying to find the flaw, the tiniest negative detail, the hiccup over which to gloat. This wasn't a conversation anymore, it was an interrogation. And she certainly wasn't interested in me or my mother or sister. She was obsessed with my father, frustrated by my skulking silence. I was unable to give her any answers at all, so she kept on pinching my cheeks. It was a way of punishing me, to the delight of the gathering of soldiers who were reduced to children once more. Noisy conversation gradually took over from the whispering and superficial friendliness with its glimpses of unvoiced resentments. I found it all so oppressive that I had an irresistible urge to return to the Euphrates and its banks lined with mischievous children.

Saad came and sat next to me to show me how to eat the traditional dish his mother had made: tashreeb, the poor man's dish that my father loved. It consisted of an Arab bread called khubz, and green onions and lamb in gravy. There was no cutlery, so you had to fold over some bread to pinch a bite of meat and onion. The dessert was slices of watermelon that you had to eat noisily. And lastly came the obligatory cardamom tea.

My uncles Khaled and Tarek stayed only as long as courtesy required. I noticed that they avoided Bibi Samiya, never even looking at her.

At dusk, I started to feel anxious—the anxiety of a child accustomed to the constant racket of city life. The silence bothered me. My sister had stayed in Baghdad and I was alone with my uncles and Bibi Samiya in a very basic house. There were hardly any toys in Fallujah, children made do with whatever was at hand. Many of them were happy running behind an old cart wheel, directing it with a stick. I was impatient to get back to Baghdad.

Once again, Saad suggested I go with him, to the kitchen this time. We sat on the floor, and he took the magazine for his revolver from his jacket. I didn't immediately understand what I was seeing. Saad sat in silence as he handled the cartridge, unscrewing it and spreading the black powder into a sinuous line on the floor. Then he turned out the light and flicked on his lighter next to the powder. Small explosions gave off sparks that snaked across the kitchen, like magical fairyland lights in the shadows of my anxiety. Saad smiled. And so did I, already imagining telling my friends about this.

That night we slept on the terrace. The Fallujah sky was clear and twinkling, donkeys brayed, and dogs or wolves howled at the moon. I gazed up at the Milky Way for the first time, the belly of the sky opening onto a multitude of stars and glimmers of hope. I took out the list of names my father had written and read it again. Samiya didn't feature on it at all.

In the morning the list had disappeared.

––––––––

I was woken by the rooster's crow and the call to prayer in the nearby mosque. The muezzin sounded so close that I pictured him at the foot of my makeshift bed. I inhaled the morning sky and realized that this brief trip to the countryside was coming to an end. I couldn't wait to get back to the bustle of the city. Breakfast was taken in silence: a mixture of sesame oil and date molasses with bread and sweet tea. I ate everything without a word and waited, ready. While I said goodbye to everyone on the doorstep, Saad maneuvered the car along the narrow street. Then I climbed into the car and waved at my other uncles. Bibi Samiya muttered something I didn't make out.

Perhaps a prayer for our journey. Perhaps something worse.

Destination Baghdad. Uncle Saad didn't breathe a word on the journey, but he kept watching me out of the corner of his eye. Had he rifled through my things in the night? So where had my list gone? I didn't dare ask him. Being back in the chaos of Baghdad was a relief but I also had a sense of shame. I'd noticed a bitterness in my uncles, a profound resentment toward Baghdadis. This age-old defiance had clearly created a bottomless rift between the two cities that stood only forty miles apart. And in between was the sinister Abu Ghraib prison, like a frontier. We stopped close to it and, seeing the barbed wire around its perimeter, I found myself imagining the inmates in their cells, dreaming of escape.

I too was looking for escape—from boredom. In the distance I recognized my cousin Omar's American car and its musical horn. He and Uncle Saad kept their distance from each other and barely even said hello. I felt I was being exchanged for a ransom. Before leaving, they parted as they'd greeted each other, without making eye contact.

"*Fimallah*, Euphrates, as we say here. It means 'Allah protect you.' And don't forget to give the message to your father," Saad said as he walked away.

Omar was chatty and relaxed, the exact opposite of Saad. As he drove, he turned down the music to ask me questions.

"Did you have a good time there?"

"Yes, it was great. I was even allowed to carry a real pistol."

"What? Shit, those guys in Fallujah!" Omar growled before turning the radio up again.

His words revealed the reciprocal of the resentment I'd witnessed: a city dweller's contempt for country folk. From my very first days in Iraq, I'd felt caught between these two adult worlds, with a sense that I had to referee. Luckily, Omar—with his cigarette between his lips—brushed aside my thoughts with another question.

"Do you want an ice cream? I know the best ice-cream maker in Baghdad."

We soon parked in the Mansour district, one of the most upscale, commercial neighborhoods in the capital. I loved the colors and smells in the streets and felt I was coming back to life. I was also especially happy to be reunited with my mother and sister and part of my mother's family. In fact, I've never forgotten those typical Baghdad sidewalks with their zigzags of ochre-colored bricks, lined with giant date palms and flowering jasmine. In every direction there were stalls displaying treats to appeal to food lovers: gleaming potato chips, pastries made with dates and sesame molasses, Italian ice creams. Iraq was definitely the empire of indulgent eating. I didn't have a "prosperity," the word Iraqis used for a small paunch. To them, I was scrawny and therefore poor. Omar may have been as skinny as I was, but he carried his little rounded belly with pride.

We walked through the souk for a long time before reaching the ice-cream shop. Everyone ordered ice cream: apricot for me, chocolate for my sister. Then we continued walking as we licked at our cones, before going our separate ways outside the souk. I stayed with Omar, who asked me lots of questions about France, particularly the girls there. Chatting away like this, we came to a local housing project. We were soon surrounded by children my age, apparently drawn by my T-shirt and Reebok Pumps.

Omar explained to them that I'd come from France.

"Faranssa?"

"Faranssa," I mumbled.

"Mitterrane, Mitterrane!" they chanted their equivalent of the French president's name.

They smiled at me, asked me about Paris, and marveled when I demonstrated what my Reeboks did. Their amazement made me look down and I saw that they were all wearing sandals. It made me feel I'd been dropped into a melting pot of privilege as a baby. One of them, a slightly older boy, handed me some car keys.

"My car for your shoes," he offered.

They all burst out laughing. At first, I thought it was a joke but soon realized it wasn't. Noticing my embarrassment, Omar took my shoulder and waved goodbye to them, then we headed back toward the souk. As we walked, I was conscious of my lucky-in-life clothes clinging to me. I was the privileged traveler wearing sports brands, while they were shut off from the world, barefoot in their sandals. I'd believed I was poor but felt like a fool surrounded by such poverty. In France we were far from rich, yes, but we lived well. And contrary to what I'd heard so many times at home, the grass wasn't necessarily greener on the other side of the fence. Had my father sent us to Iraq for me to see this for myself? As soon as I was back at Aunt Sumaya's house, I took off my Reeboks and threw them in a closet.

We spent the end of the summer on the farm owned by Aziz, Aunt Sumaya's husband, who was passionate about horses. In this second home on the outskirts of Baghdad, Aziz had set up a stud farm for purebred Arab horses, and each of the stallions was named after one of his children. It was the first time I'd ever set foot in a stable. The staff, who were from Egypt and Sudan, spoke a different Arabic. Aziz told them to prepare a coal fire to cook a traditional dish, masgouf, a local variety of carp cooked on an open fire—just as the Sumerians used to seven thousand years ago, Aziz told me. He picked up a huge carp, a freshwater fish caught in the Tigris, opened it along its whole length, and put it into a vertical grill standing close to the fire.

While it was cooking, we were served several dishes in a wide variety of colors. Once again, I was impressed by just how much food Iraqis could eat.

A few hours later, the fish provided tender white meat with a slightly smoky taste, and Aziz doused it with lemon juice. Then I did what everyone else was doing: eating the masgouf with their fingers by pinching it between pieces of khubz and trying to avoid the saber-length bones. The meal ended with the inevitable cardamom tea, served with little pastries called mann al-sama, which means fallen from heaven—a sort of nougat rolled in white powder and sprinkled with pistachios. The last days of summer drifted by in this profusion of flavors and smells that I will never forget, like Iraq itself, which I treasured deep inside.

1989 was a year of peace. Fallujah had become my Normandy, Baghdad my Ardèche, and I returned to France with these fragments of a country. I was reunited with my father, my friends, the road with the dancing poplars, the goods trains, my shuddering bed, and the shadows on the ceiling. All I could think about was the start of the school year when I would finally be able to tell my friends stories about my summer vacation. Especially Kader.

HATEM

(Summer 1954)

THIS MEMORY of Rami's dates back to September of a turbulent year.

It was the first day of school and Rami was ten years old. On the way to school, he and Hatem were smoking Miami Blues, made in Vietnam's run-down factories. The boys' school building looked as if it was constructed in clay with shades of ochre. On rainy days the walls and ground seemed to merge.

In Mr. Fadil's class everyone watched their step. Before he began the roll call, the *mualim* adopted a severe stance in keeping with his reputation. No one escaped either his remonstrations or his heavy hand. Each pupil had to fill out a form: first name, family name, address, father's profession, favorite subject.

In the space for "father's profession" Rami wrote *professional writer.* He would have been so much happier to have put *soldier* like everyone else. Because in this garrison town being a soldier's son was the norm. But that wasn't what Rami's father was. Favorite subject: *mathematics*.

The teacher called the boys up to the blackboard one after another.

"Hatem Shakir."

Hatem stood up, looking uncomfortable, and put his hands in his pockets.

"Stand up properly, you idiot!" snapped Mr. Fadil.

Hatem stood up as straight as he could, and the teacher read his form out loud.

"Father—buffalo farmer?"

Stifled laughter around the classroom.

"Yes, buffalo farmer," Hatem replied with his eyes lowered.

"Very well, sit back down."

All the pupils looked the same; they dressed in the same way and rummaged through the same satchels and the same pencil cases. Hatem, who was almost as imposing a figure as Mr. Fadil, seemed older than the others. He was, in fact, and there was an explanation for this anomaly. And Rami knew about it.

School wasn't compulsory in Iraq in the 1950s, and in order to enroll you needed an ID card, to be on the country's census, to exist as a citizen. In a word, to be lucky. But Hatem didn't even know his date of birth. Rami was one of the lucky ones who knew where and when they were born— he also knew that Muhja had given birth at home and that his father had gone to the *baladiya*, the records office, to register his youngest son's birth and obtain a national ID card for him. That's not what happened with Hatem. His parents, who were illiterate, knew nothing about administrative procedures or the fact that these procedures were vital to life as part of society.

Hatem had been born in a far-off region and was one of the *bidoon jinsiya*, who had no nationality. Put another way, they had no papers, no rights, no work, and no education. They were the no-anything-at-alls, entitled to nothing. Stateless people. Most of them came from southern Iraq, desert regions on the border with neighboring Kuwait, and they had never been the subject of a census before modern Iraq. For a great majority of them it was now too late to become citizens. They'd missed the boat. They didn't exist. Had they ever?

Unusually, some *bidoon* had a roof over their heads. Hatem and his family lived in an outlying shantytown, Al Rahmaniya. The name means "mercy," and its inhabitants needed some. Hatem's childhood had been one of utmost destitution. Instead of going to school, he'd been responsible for grazing his father's buffalo near the Euphrates. The muddy animals moved slowly, almost gracefully, as they meekly followed their master. Hatem was known locally as the *tabur*, the singing reaper, because he sang to his buffalo from morning till night and cut down tall grasses to feed them. When he had the time, he rested near the bridge and jumped into the river to bury watermelons or clean off the dirt from moving to new pastureland. It was here that he'd met Rami, here that he'd saved him from drowning, here that the younger boy had suggested he enroll at school, and here that a pact of friendship had been sealed.

In order to attend school, he'd first had to convince his father, who had only ever been a buffalo farmer and couldn't care less about school. He sold his geymar, a sort of white butter highly prized by Iraqis, and this was what kept his family alive. He made it himself, simmering buffalo milk for a long time before skimming off the cream and leaving it to stand and ferment for hours, even days. For breakfast Iraqis put this white butter on toasted bread and drizzled it with date molasses.

"I'm filling Iraqi stomachs. Now that's a job!" Hatem's father had replied when his son had asked if he could go to school.

Each day that went by with no school or lessons, Hatem drew closer to his father's lot in life.

"School will never get you a real job! Reading? Writing? Whatever for? Forget it!" his father insisted.

But fate, with the help of an uncle, would smile on Hatem. This uncle, who was a close acquaintance of someone at the *baladiya*, could arrange for Hatem to exist in the eyes of the state, and could therefore enroll him in school. An incredible stroke of luck. A turning point in his life. Having an education was something of a miracle for these families that the state refused to recognize. Over time, with persistent persuasion, Hatem's father reluctantly conceded. On just one condition: Hatem would still be available to tend to the buffalo.

The procedure seemed simple enough. To allow his son to be born a second time, Hatem's father needed to find two people who would testify in court. These two witnesses would be the aforementioned uncle and Rami's father.

At the registry office they settled on March 5 as Hatem's birthday. Now they just needed to establish the year. Even though he looked fourteen, they opted to say he was ten, which would be better for him to catch up at school. That's how Hatem, administratively speaking, was born on March 5, 1944. The two witnesses took the oath in front of a judge at the *baladiya*. And Hatem was now ten years old.

The following year, he ended up with Rami in the final year of primary school in Mr. Fadil's class. Some forty pupils learned their lessons under the leadership of this all-powerful schoolmaster: reading, mathematics, geography, drawing, and sports. The man you must not look in the eye. He wore small round glasses, never smiled, and was absolutely intransigent with his pupils, whom he referred to as "the animals" with no hint of affection. Hatem was often the black sheep, sometimes the scapegoat. He lagged far behind the others because he'd been admitted to the final year of primary school when he couldn't read or write. Wielding his large stick, the teacher regularly asked Hatem to get up, stand with his back to the wall and spread his hands to take his punishment. Hatem knew nothing, never prepared for lessons, and didn't do his homework. He was by far the most substandard and insolent boy in the class, even the whole establishment. So the teacher beat his hands at every opportunity. Hatem held out his upturned hands and closed his eyes, ready to take these beatings, which he accepted as an inevitability that had to be laughed off, come summer or winter. In fact, he preferred winter, when his frozen fingers felt less pain. Despite the abuse he suffered at school, he kept smiling. Every time he was punished by Mr. Fadil, he put a brave face on it, in his own clumsy way—it was enough to send Mr. Fadil into a fury.

Rami had also been given the treatment, even though he was so good at mathematics—perhaps too much so for the teacher's liking. Mr. Fadil had ignored the fact that Rami had named math as his favorite subject, and the boy grasped ideas so quickly at school that Fadil became suspicious of him.

One morning when everyone was working on a group exercise, Rami was the first to give the correct answer.

"How did you get it? Where are your workings?" Mr. Fadil shouted.

"I don't know," replied Rami, unable to explain that he'd done the sums in his head, and the process came naturally to him.

"You're a cheat!"

Mr. Fadil decided to punish him in front of the whole class. He beat his hand with a metal ruler for many long minutes. Three rounds. Unlike Hatem, Rami didn't manage to keep smiling.

From that moment on, Rami and Hatem were the black sheep of the class. Rami never raised his hand again.

One day Rami and Hatem walked across the playground to take refuge behind a low wall where they couldn't be seen. They were so well hidden that they blended into the clay wall. Hatem took out a pack of cigarettes and almost before they'd lit one Rami smothered a cry of alarm. Mr. Fadil had surreptitiously followed them to foil them. Impossible to deny the evidence. Hatem turned around, threw down the cigarette, and ground it out in front of the teacher.

"What were you doing behind the wall here?" Mr. Fadil asked.

"Nothing, Mr. Fadil," Rami stammered.

"We were smoking," Hatem intervened, looking Fadil right in the eye.

"What were you smoking?"

"Cigarettes, just cigarettes," Rami replied.

"Give me the packet right now and go back to the playground," the teacher said sharply.

At the end of the afternoon the superintendent, a sinister great colossus of a man, came to see Hatem. He was suspended from school for three days for insubordination and breaking the rules. Rami, who wasn't investigated, didn't understand—after all, he too had been caught red-handed. It was easy to find people who were treated more favorably than you, but occasionally you joined the ranks of the privileged.

Once the sentence was passed, Hatem was sent to his uncle who ran one of Fallujah's small businesses. A little stall with a few household items: sugar, matches, cigarettes, tea. Hatem may have remembered no part of his school lessons, but he knew the price of everything. Thirty centimes for a pack of cigarettes. Five for matches. Eighty per kilo of sugar. And, a great luxury, two dinars per kilo of tea. As Hatem saw it, this was where the class difference lay: While townspeople bought a kilo of sugar and one of tea, country folk could barely afford one cigarette.

"What happened, Hatem? Why aren't you at school?" asked his uncle, surprised.

"It's Mr. Fadil, he doesn't want me around."

"Really? Well, I'll go see him. You won't have any more problems, understand?"

For the next three days Hatem worked in the fields with his father, who used the opportunity to try to persuade him to give up. He reminded him that they had a roof over their heads, buffalo, and a business, and that they were needed by society.

But the uncle kept insisting, "Your son needs a decent future!"

"I don't care if he can read or write, he belongs in the fields!" Hatem's father always replied.

On the third day of this suspension, the uncle went to see Mr. Fadil, accompanied by a high-ranking official from the *baladiya*. Voices were raised between the two men and threats were made to the *mualim*.

"The *baladiya* could cast an eye over your teaching methods," threatened the uncle, "and that might compromise your career!"

The following week, Hatem returned to school, escorted by his uncle, who lectured him along the way, pointing menacingly at his face. Rami thought he'd never see his friend at school again, however Hatem returned to his place at the back of the class without a glance at the other children or a word to his friend. But there was a new glint in his eye, a glint of determination.

Shortly after that, things changed. Mr. Fadil's attitude altered: He was no longer the same man, he stopped hounding Hatem, the hostility had disappeared. Rami's friend suddenly seemed to grow in stature. Uncharacteristically, Hatem concentrated on the blackboard that Mr. Fadil smothered with equations in his algebra class. It was then that Rami realized his friend had chosen school over the fields.

The year ended in the same way and Hatem no longer worried about the *mualim*'s angry outbursts. Now he had to survive out of school when his father sent him off to tend to the buffalo as much as possible. And then one morning, when Hatem was starting his umpteenth day leading them to pasture, he decided to put a stop to it. No more trailing around fields, putting up with jeers from the other children, hearing all sorts of bird's names being called when he walked past. Hatem said no to his father and confronted the tyranny of the peasant community. He was going to learn to read and write, and become someone. Of course, his father protested vehemently.

"I need to live," Hatem told him.

"You need a job."

"Well, I'll find a job!"

"Are you sure?"

"I don't know, but saying 'I don't know' is halfway to science. Mr. Fadil said so."

"And do you know what your father says? Go look after the buffalo!"

Hatem squared up to his father, looked him in the eye, and refused once and for all. He wouldn't be taking the buffalo to pasture again, summer or winter. He wouldn't be going to school to please his uncle anymore. He would be going for his own sake, and one day he would make his way to the capital, which would give him an opportunity. Because Baghdad was the center of the universe. And it was a place where you could dream. He promised himself he would go there with Rami, his longtime friend, and together they fostered dreams of a better life.

He could never have imagined that one day Baghdad would fall.

THE GHOST

(September 1990)

I JOINED my fourth-grade class one week late; my sister and I had both missed a few days of school.

"Oh, it must be a ghost!" Kader exclaimed when he saw me.

Because yes, we really had vanished. We'd gone to Iraq from one day to the next. It was urgent: The truce might not last.

The pupils in my new class had all sorts of fathers: a train driver, a doctor, a plumber, an engineer, an IT specialist, a soccer coach, a certified public accountant, a police officer, a mechanic. Mine bore little relation to all this normality, but he still worked. As I looked at the form I had to fill out, I regretted having lied in previous years.

When I'd first started school, I'd been keen to blend into the background. As soon as I walked through the school gate, I tried to hide how different my family was by taking refuge in confabulation. How could I write *postcard salesman on the forecourt of Notre-Dame*? Who would understand the fact that plainclothes policemen regularly arrested him? So I invented professions for him based on what I knew about him: He'd studied sociology, dabbled in politics, and traveled to a number of countries. And I created different profiles for him thanks to the various snippets of conversation I'd overheard. In first grade, when Mrs. Bruchon asked me about this, I'd said *politician* and had been gratified with a smile in return. In second grade I'd opted for *sociologist*. In third grade, *import-export trader*. School had become a refuge where I could lie and feel normal, closer to the others.

Yes, we had a car, a Peugeot or a Mercedes, depending on the contracts my father secured. Obviously, we went to the Côte d'Azur for vacations. Of course, we were frequent flyers. Did my father ever take me to his office? No but, you know, he traveled a lot.

In fourth grade I decided to tell the truth. I wrote in black on white: *postcard salesman*. I almost added: "Father sacrificing himself for his family. Honorable work all the same. Sure, could have done better. Long university career not completed. Started studying sociology at college in Poitiers, gave up because of the demands of family life."

I didn't dare. Who'd have believed me? Wouldn't people have made fun of me?

I felt relieved. Relieved that I'd finally revealed a grain of truth.

———

Mrs. Girard asked if I would agree to tell everyone what I'd seen in Iraq. Before I had time to reply Kader accepted on my behalf.

"Go on," he said. "Tell us about your shady country, ghost boy!"

Sniggering around the classroom.

So, I went ahead. What did my classmates know about the country? Nothing. And that nothing meant everything to me. That nothing was my origins, my story, my family tree. That nothing was my discovery of my father's hometown. Fallujah, on the banks of the Euphrates, which had given me my name. I started to describe the place: clean and green and dusty, not as illustrious as Baghdad, no, but still charming. In Fallujah I met people whose lives I'd spent so much time imagining—lots of uncles and aunts, many more cousins. I felt so alone in France, but there I'd been inundated with new faces. I had a big family at last.

I described the supermodern airport built by the French, the hundreds of open arms welcoming us, the American cars, the ice cream savored on the corner of Mansour Street, the huge houses with flower-filled gardens, the date palms as tall as the Eiffel Tower, the watermelons as long as summer. I kept to myself the fact that you had to whisper there, that you couldn't say the dictator's name out loud, that some people kept a watchful eye on others, that my father hadn't been able to join us—and that I didn't know why. It was my Iraq, and that particular Iraq was happy in spite of everything. There was nothing middling in that distant Middle Eastern country. It was big. It wasn't "shady." It was a secret. It had become my other country. In Iraq we had as many varieties of dates as there were cheeses in France. There was even a very rare blue date that fruits every ten years. I added that no one should ever forget where they're from, that I wasn't forgetting but I was having a hard time of it. I didn't know what to do with this feeling of being an imposter when you're born in France, by chance or out of luck, the son of a political activist, a refugee, or an immigrant—it didn't really matter at the end of the day. I didn't know how to accommodate the idea that I was privileged in the eyes of my own family over there.

When I'd finished, I sat back down with a scrape of my chair on the floor, and felt I'd said too much.

A long silence descended over the room. Then, much to my surprise, Kader started clapping, once, twice, three times, joined by the rest of the class. This moment of grace showed me it was possible to feel great pride and great embarrassment at the same time. During the applause, Kader turned and gave me a thumbs-up. Soon the usual classroom chatter resumed as if nothing had happened. I was back among the others. A ghost accepted and honored for a description that had lasted a good fifteen minutes.

Every opportunity was a good one for gleaning information from Mrs. Girard's soporific lessons. Instead of teaching us history, she told it to us in stories, often overlapping them with her own. I always liked the earnestness of those times when, instead of the school curriculum, she diverted into her own life.

One day, one of the girls dared to ask her how old she was. By way of a reply, Mrs. Girard entangled herself in an anecdote that went on for at least ten minutes, before concluding, "Sixty-two, my dear."

Then she paused before adding, with a degree of solemnity, something that came from the depths of her soul, like a sigh of personal truth, perhaps the only one she ever gave us: "You'll see, life goes by in the blink of an eye."

These words of Mrs. Girard's were still reverberating in my mind as my sister and I went home from school. And they would soon assume their full meaning.

"Bibi Samiya has died, be kind to your dad," my mother told us on the landing outside our apartment.

Skulking behind an impenetrable wall, my father clearly didn't want to talk about it. He opened a bottle of wine and put his Walkman earphones over his head. When the alcohol caught up with him, I heard him constantly repeating words that seemed to echo distant memories: "You're nothing. You're nothing now. You're nothing to me now. With our souls and with our blood, we'll serve you, dear comrade! And we'll cross the bridge. And we'll lie in wait for them. And we'll drive them out of the country!"

I didn't yet understand these strange pronouncements, neither the damage of his childhood nor the revolutionary sentiments.

REVOLUTION

(July 1958)

MY FATHER'S political life started with a misunderstanding.

1958 was a year of sound and fury. Events that would surely have been unimaginable the year before unfolded and whipped emotions into a frenzy. Rami and Hatem were still a separate unit from the rest of their class. They had a form of suffering in common: being wiped from existence. Rami was dismissed by his father, abused by his stepmother, and ignored by his brothers. Hatem, the *bidoon*, stood up to his father, the buffalo farmer. The two friends helped each other nurture their hope of changing their destinies. They often found themselves dreaming of someday securing a prestigious residency at Al-Mustansiriya University in Baghdad to study elevated subjects. In the meantime, they'd battled to survive middle school and then high school, and to get the better of the circumstances to which they'd been banished.

Hatem and Rami had never seen the capital. That was probably why Hatem came up with the idea of a getaway trip one day, and Rami immediately agreed to it. One of the local buses went from Fallujah to Baghdad for just a quarter of a dinar. They didn't need much: a bit of small change and a bit of courage. The plan embedded itself in their minds and continued to mature over the next few days. Until Monday, July 14, 1958.

They had agreed to meet early that morning, before the start of lessons. Just one hour of traveling lay between them and a whole other world. At nine o'clock sharp a minibus crammed with workmen dropped them at the gates to the capital. Baghdad proved radically different from the world young Hatem and Rami had left behind: It melded the exotic with the familiar, the modern with the traditional. The Tigris, which meandered through the capital, was as wide and magisterial as the Euphrates, but its silent black waters flowed more slowly between gardens so luxuriant they'd make an angel blush. They followed the river and discovered a dense, solid profusion of eucalyptus, orange trees, and date palms whose elegant crowns swayed gracefully to the whims of the wind.

To anyone from the countryside, Baghdad was another planet. You could talk about anything there: In cafés political ranting came face-to-face with poets' recitations. Several places allowed men and women to spend time together, sometimes holding hands. And yet Baghdad was a victim of its own size and of a fundamental jealousy. The city of peace was experiencing troubled times because of widespread instability in the Middle East—particularly in Egypt, where Nasser had overturned power, nationalized the Suez Canal, and established the United Arab Republic. The war with the West was starting, and the Soviets were stepping onto the political chessboard in a region where there was no king or queen to staunch the steam powering this runaway train.

Rami and Hatem came to the top of Al Rashid Street, the most modern street in the city. Its endless big hotels, travel agencies, movie theaters, and clothing stores, its jewelers and bookstores all stood alongside the same modest little shops as in Fallujah. Surrounded by this assorted, multicolored population, the two buddies felt unexpectedly lightheaded.

"You want a smoke?" suggested Rami.

They were quietly smoking their Miami Blues when they were surrounded by an exuberant crowd. Men in red-and-black checkered kaffiyehs and a few women in abayas, alongside men in Western suits and ties, had appeared as if by magic, chanting slogans. The crowd was swelling and becoming more compact, and it was soon impossible to plow through it. To avoid being crushed, Rami and Hatem had to walk along with it. Then they suddenly recognized a face among the demonstrators. They rubbed their eyes in disbelief: Mr. Fadil, the man who never smiled, was there with an unexpectedly passionate expression on his face.

Staying not far from him along Al Rashid Street, Rami and Hatem couldn't get over what they were witnessing. Instead of reciting equations, Mr. Fadil was bellowing slogans with the revolutionaries. The boys may not have known anything about politics, but they could tell that something exceptional was taking place before their eyes. As they marched alongside their "comrades," Rami even caught himself adopting their unfamiliar chants. Cries of "Take your weapons, citizens! Form your battalions!" from "La Marseillaise" mingled with "To the red banner of our sacred fatherland we will forever be wholeheartedly true!" from the Soviet Union's anthem. And then over and above these refrains the crowd started to chorus what seemed like their own song of allegiance: "With our souls and with our blood we will serve you, dear comrade Qasim! Down with the imperialist feudal system! With our souls and with our blood…"

Moments later the crowd was spilling through the streets, celebrating the fall of the monarchy with unprecedented fervor. Rami and Hatem were watching a turning point in history. Iraq would be changed forever.

The royal palace had been besieged at dawn, and young King Faisal, his uncle who was regent, and the much-despised prime minister had been arrested. Then in a flash of anger a soldier had opened fire on the royal party, killing every member of the family. The republic was proclaimed.

Later in the day, the leader of the new state, Abd al-Karim Qasim, announced the end of colonialism and imperialism. What should have been good news was now tainted with the terrible smell of blood and the bitter taste of a disappointed love for the monarchy, which had led to murderous fanaticism. A heavy veil of silence descended over the country. On July 14, 1958, the regime became revolutionary, parliament became a revolutionary tribunal, and everyone claimed to be a revolutionary. The strict Mr. Fadil was calling for revolution. Rami couldn't help rebelling too and Hatem was euphoric.

When the marching came to a stop in what would later be known as Liberation Square, an animated Rami put a protective arm around Hatem's shoulders.

"My companion in revolution, let me warn you, we may well end up in prison for having these thoughts."

"Would you like a cigarette, comrades?" came a voice from somewhere behind them.

On the far sidewalk a clean-shaven Mr. Fadil was watching them indulgently. He greeted his former students, then took a pack of cigarettes from his pocket and offered it to them. Night was drawing in. The chanting was still going on in the distance: "With our souls and with our blood we will serve you, dear comrade Qasim! Down with the imperialist feudal system! With our souls and with our blood…"

That was how these words became imprinted on Rami's mind. On that day he signed an unspoken pact while he, Hatem, and Mr. Fadil smoked a cigarette that tasted of revolution.

WAR IN RECESS

(January 1991)

MY OWN political life was prompted by a taunt, by disappointment with a friend.

The last few months had been a long nightmare.

During our second trip to Iraq, my Ardèche had fallen right before our eyes. On August 2, 1990, Saddam Hussein invaded Kuwait. The frontiers were closed, and we were trapped. I thought I'd never see France again. After acrimonious negotiations, we and the other rare foreigners in the country were saved at the last moment thanks to a human corridor to Jordan.

The man whose name I'd been told never to say was now on every television screen. Everyone was talking about him. Iraq had broken out of our small apartment and was being discussed left, right, and center. Yes, Saddam Hussein was being criticized for his invasion, but my father was incensed.

"It's all over for Iraq," he announced that first day.

Six months later the response certainly was particularly violent. Baghdad was bombed. That evening, we all watched the TV news. Iraqi anti-aircraft fire slashed through the night sky. Green flashes, explosions, and then appalling images the following morning. It was with that war that my father started drinking again.

He stood in front of the TV, roaring, "Go on, my brothers!"

I've never found the words to describe what I felt that day, and I probably never will.

The Iraq that I'd constructed after my first trip came tumbling down overnight. War was destroying my dream of a prosperous Normandy.

A bad headache from that evening. My mother put her hand on my forehead to gauge my temperature. She didn't believe in this imaginary sickness for a moment. I was sick because of the war, but she didn't want to hear about it. After a restless night of watching Baghdad's dark skies ripped open by anti-aircraft fire, I had to go to school and face everyone else. Iraq wasn't an unknown entity now, it was the floor show. Everyone was talking about the fireworks in the sky. My classmates stared at me: I was the only Iraqi in school, maybe in the city, all of France even. Wherever I took shelter—in a corner of the playground or under the covered area—people peered at me. I didn't know how to handle it. My friends came over to me in the playground, surrounding me, wanting to see my reaction. I stiffened and the conversation didn't go as I'd expected.

"Did you see the war on TV? It was like a movie!" whooped Kader.

"Except it's not a movie, Kader," I replied coldly.

"Are you kidding? It's better than *Star Wars*!"

A burst of laughter from the others. I could feel my anger rising, my pulse thumped in my temples.

I'd naively hoped for moral support from an Arab "brother." In vain.

"The Americans fucked you guys up!" Kader continued, sniggering. "They're the most powerful army in the world, you know."

Kader was my first disappointment and would be my last. That day I realized just how violent words can be. Not words intended to crush or annihilate, but faux-innocent words that cut deep. I thought about my family being bombed. Kader was still laughing. I balled my fists. He kept going. So I threw myself at him. Never before had I fought for a political reason, a betrayal, an injustice.

———

Mrs. Crespi, the school principal, summoned me to her office. When I explained the situation, she sat down beside me, watching me all the time.

"Can I suggest we start from the beginning again, calmly. I'm listening. What's really going on?" she asked.

I explained the unbearable situation: my family being bombed, my sleepless father standing staring at the TV, my mother who thought she recognized a cousin among the prisoners. Not forgetting those flashes of light in the dark, the fires from bombs that had given me nightmares the night before, the anger and powerlessness, my hope for some empathy that I hadn't found, not on TV or at school. Tears had even stopped tasting of salt. Did I regret what I did? Of course. I shouldn't have gotten carried away. After all, no one knew Iraq. Neither did I, as it happened. But that simple insult had made me feel like part of an ignored minority enduring the stupidity of an ignorant major-ity. I'd found it hard. Unfair? Yes, that's it—unfair. So I'd bunched my fists. Kader shouldn't have done it. Iraq was dying right in front of us. My distant backwater wasn't a joke. You shouldn't laugh about it. It wasn't a movie. It was all real. And it stank of death.

The principal nodded slowly, smiled at me, and then started talking. She said she too was thinking about Iraq, she expressed compassion for my family, and admitted she was afraid of a global conflict and a humanitarian disaster. She wiped away a tear from under her glasses.

It was in Mrs. Crespi's office that I found the support I'd wanted from my classmates. She promised she wouldn't say anything to my parents and that she would visit us at home for news of our family in Iraq.

After that, I often saw her crying with my mother and father, right up until the end of Operation Desert Storm.

Thirty-six countries destroyed mine that winter. My father took to drinking a bottle of wine every night.

And I was given the job of buying them.

———

The sun had almost disappeared, leaving behind a necklace of clouds in reds and mauves across the sky. I roamed the sidewalk, crouched on my skateboard and hurtled down the street with its dancing poplars. At the crossroads at the bottom, the predatory smile of a furniture salesman beamed from a billboard. The grocer opposite was arranging his fruit stalls. I waited for him to go back into the store, checked all around, and slipped discreetly inside. With shame clinging to every part of me, I walked around the shelves of candy and past the refrigerators of chilled drinks to the small room—and it too was discreet—at the back of the store: the wine section. I took a bottle of Côtes du Rhône and put it on the counter. The owner always looked amused by my embarrassment.

I'd already been afraid of my father sometimes. And I'd been afraid *for* him sometimes as well. When he was sober, he avoided confrontations as if to avoid his own violence. And with me, that violence had taken the form of a slap. But when my father started drinking, nothing around him seemed to exist, his paranoia took control, and he couldn't see anything. He let his inner turmoil take over. And I cursed the bottle of wine that woke his demons. In those days, my father often brought his work and the cops home with him in the evenings. His anger became increasingly difficult to control the more alcohol he drank. I was well aware that intoxication never traveled alone: It kept bad company. Like on that evening.

A small group of us were heading to the Métro on our way home after a get-together for Iraqi dissidents—a fringe group that was opposed to Saddam Hussein but also criticized the American and UN war that looked inevitable. In a large private-hire room in the Montparnasse neighborhood, we'd spent the evening debating, laughing, crying, and drinking. And my father had had that one glass too many.

We took the last Métro from a station called Gaîté—it means "cheerfulness."

When we stepped into the carriage my father tripped. Every time I go over it in my head, my blood freezes. Every time. I was nine years old, and I remember every detail as if it was yesterday. My father made his way to the end of the carriage, turned down a flip-up seat, slumped onto it, and took out a cigarette. Two men opposite him looked him up and down. They too appeared to be a little drunk. After a while one of them came over to my father to ask him to put out his cigarette. When he got no reaction, the man stayed standing defiantly in front of him. The second guy joined his friend so there were now two of them facing my father who just sat there, not even looking up at them.

The subway carriage was erased.

I could visualize the rising tension. It danced around us, snaked up to my father, sniffed at the other two men, tickled their nostrils, eyed me, smiled at me, winked, clicked its fingers…

Saint-Placide station. The Métro warned that the doors were about to close with its ringing sound, like the bell in a boxing ring.

As soon as the doors were closed my father jumped up and headbutted the chin of the man directly in front of him. The man fell heavily and tried to catch the central pole to break his fall. My father straightened up again, his body relaxed but his eyes blazing with an anger I would never have thought possible of him. My heart pounded wildly.

"Dad!" I wailed. "Please! Stop!"

As he readied himself for another attack, I heard my mother screaming behind me. Everything in that carriage was screaming, my eardrums, my mother and sister, my father's friends. Three wild animals out of control. The seconds crawled by like hours. Unable to stop the fray, Iraqi friends from the meeting kept a safe distance. The whole carriage was filled with our anguish. My father was still fighting with the second man, a more imposing opponent than the first. I saw him rip the man's scarf, swing his fist forward. Tears had now taken over from the screams. I couldn't breathe. My lungs were burning. I wanted someone to do something. No one from our group intervened. Only my mother stepped forward, arms spread to form a wall, as if breaking up a scrap between her children. Time stood still, we were buffeted by the movements of the subway train and terrified by the punches flying. Then it all stopped at Odéon station. The train stayed on the platform and four men came into the carriage, clearly plainclothes policemen. They separated my father and the other two men.

"What happened here?" asked one of the officers.

"They attacked my husband!" cried my mother. "Maybe because we're Muslim."

"But we're Muslim too! We're Pakistani," the other two replied.

My father said nothing. But I got it: Iraq was falling apart so badly that it was destroying my father. His drinking, his violence, everything was because of the war that was insidiously worming its way into our lives.

Olfactory memory is the most emotional and the most arbitrary. It catches us by surprise with a snatch of a smell, a meeting, a place. It pops up with no warning. And that night I rediscovered the smell of sulfur that had followed me the first time I'd taken the Métro. Ever since, that smell has always reminded me of war and its venom.

ROOM 219

(August 4, 2019)

IT WAS raining. I closed the window on the muskiness of wet soil. The smell of rain pervaded the room, and a slight breeze wafted the last wisp of hair on my father's head. There was nothing left now of the fighter of old with his arms like a sailor's, his rock-hard belly, and his long curly hair. He didn't take the Métro anymore. Now he just looked like an ageless, cancerous, forgetful man kept alive by an oxygen cylinder. He was wearing a blue-and-white hospital gown, open over his scrawny back that was hunched by the years. I stifled my tears.

"And no one in the Métro helped me?" he asked, lost in thought.

No, no one had helped him. His friends had kept their distance that evening. After that, they'd drifted away, staying in touch less and less. An absence of a few days, a few weeks, and then the last thirty years.

Outside, the sky cleared and the sun broke through again. Rays of light poured into the room, further highlighting my father's frail frame. He looked at me. Had he noticed I was watching him? I didn't know what to do.

Then he announced, with a note of reproach in his voice, "You must be brave, mine son."

Mine son. His accent, his grammatical mistakes, his almost perfect French were now a source of pride to me. They bore witness to his story, his journey, his individuality. That wasn't at all how I'd felt as a child. Now I was ashamed of having been ashamed. So I told him. I told him about my little private wound, the small humiliation on my conscience.

THAT ACCENT

(March 1991)

AS A child I wanted to mask my parents' accent.

They spoke a distinctive French, their pronunciation wasn't like other immigrant parents'. My mother didn't roll her *r*'s. She hardened them, reinforced them, exaggerated them. And she spaced out her syllables. So, for example, she said *farrrrrrroot* for fruit and *eight-ah farrrrrrrancs* for eight francs. My sister and I were always correcting her. It made no difference. Her accent stuck. By contrast, my father spoke better, sometimes even quite formal French. *Almost* perfect French. And the *almost* lay in word inversions that gave him away, revealing distant origins. The imperfection was apparent to the ear in the illogicality of some expressions that gave away the scent of exile. One of the things he said was "that does mean not" and he had an annoying habit of feminizing some masculine words. My parents coped very well, but they were hostage to a language with a stigmatizing accent and so, afraid they might unsettle people, they even apologized.

———

My parents were very polite. My father a little too much so: His whole face lit up amicably when he greeted someone. His expression changed completely and became an open window onto his extreme courtesy. During the briefest interaction, he raised his eyebrows, pursed his lips in agreement, and tilted his head (too much) as a mark of respect. He positioned himself below the other person. He single-handedly embodied the Iraqi saying that I would hear much later and that I wouldn't yet have understood: "I put you on my head"—a sign of complete respect and submission, as a matter of principle. Perhaps this courtesy was a safeguard. Being discreet to keep violence from erupting, to avoid revealing the true self. For many years I believed that this discretion was a weakness. I later realized that it was a strength on the outer borders of the deep-seated anger felt by every exile. This gnawing anger could erupt at any moment in my parents, and the discretion they displayed was merely a rampart for the rage corralled on the tips of their tongues.

We were not to talk about this latent violence at home. The incident in the Métro had heightened my social anxiety. But we had to move on, shut the rage away in a box. That day, I had learned that shame could sometimes be a gauge of buried anger.

———

It was nearly time for my appointment with the dentist. I could already smell stress-inducing wafts of cloves.

"You must be brave, Euphrates," my father said before my appointment, but the well-meant encouragement was a disaster to my ears: He'd used the word for a brave girl: *courageuse*.

"It's *courageux* for a boy, Dad."

"Yes, mine son, be *courageux*."

Dr. Fernand's office was on the first floor of a white building next door to a branch of Micromania, my dream store. This proximity helped me find the courage to face the dentist at least once a year. My mother and I had made a deal: If I agreed to open my mouth and be treated, she promised I could spend some time in Micromania—her personal oil of cloves, her way of soothing my fear and pain.

The dentist's office occupied two rooms with green-and-white walls: the waiting room and the torture room. A few houseplants battled to add some cheer to the reception area and the threshold to the room where a monster on wheels was revving up to grind my damaged tooth. Dr. Fernand had been caring for me since I was very little and hadn't softened up much over the years. At the end of each appointment, he solemnly shook my hand with a "Well done, you were a man." It was my job to contain my tears till we were outside to prove him right.

That day was especially difficult. The dentist performed a root canal on one of my teeth under anesthetic. Acute pain, tears kept in check for the dentist's laconic pronouncement.

―――――――

As promised, my mother, my sister, and I then went into the wonderful dream store next door to the site of my suffering. The video-game chain had regular "discovery" days when customers were invited to try out new products before they came to the market. It was one of those days, and there were crowds of people. I knew the place by heart: to the left of the entrance, the checkouts; to the right, countless rows of video games stretched to the far end. Between the two, sales assistants in blue-and-yellow T-shirts strolled the aisles. They looked like big kids. I wove my way to the counter to ask for a ticket, the precious sesame that allocated ten minutes to anyone who wanted to try out a game. I opted for the blue hedgehog that everyone called Sonic.

Twenty minutes later, there still wasn't a single place free. Arwa was throwing her hands in every direction and my mother kept sighing. Losing patience, she started buttonholing the sales staff who were chatting among themselves at the counter.

"Well, can't you see it's busy, ma'am? Just have to wait like everyone else, okay?" one of them replied rather churlishly.

"Yes, sir, but was waited twenty minutes alrrrrready," my mother replied, exasperated.

Whenever she readied herself for an argument, her accent thickened. The salesman's amused expression sharpened my mother's sense that she was being disrespected. But she continued to protest, regardless. The mocking glances morphed into laughter and the laughter into grimacing.

My mother fell into the trap. Her complaint, legitimate as it was, became an affront and we were now the prey in the lion's den. All eyes were locked on us. We were surrounded by lions baring their fangs.

"Calling your manager!" my mother eventually insisted.

"Of course, ma'am. I'll 'calling' him, ma'am," sniggered a salesman with a mullet and tattooed arms.

We were stunned by his condescending tone. My sister and I were terrified of what would inevitably happen next. We knew what our mother was like, and the shame that always went everywhere with her. We were going to draw attention to ourselves.

When the manager appeared, the show already had quite an audience.

"Yes, ma'am, what's the problem?" he asked.

"It's that man over there, not talking to me properly."

"Which one, ma'am?"

"Him, with the yellow eyes!" she shouted, pointing to a salesman with pale eyes.

Laughter from the crowd. My mother often transliterated Iraqi expressions: In Arabic "yellow eyes" means hazel eyes.

The laughing proved more devastating than gunshots. It cut through my flesh, ravaged my internal organs, destroyed me.

"And what did the man with the yellow eyes say, ma'am?" the manager asked sarcastically, instead of calming things down.

"Boooooo, that's right, ma'am, I'm the one with the yellow eyes, hi there!" joked the salesman, turning for approval from his coworkers and then the impromptu audience.

"You know I don't speak French good," my mother said defensively, also crushed by the arsenal of laughter coming from all around the store.

"Of course, ma'am, I have yellow eyes. Thank you, ma'am, okay. See you soon. Go on, scram, you can go now, I have stuff to do."

I turned to my sister. She was just as ashamed as I was and kept her head down. I knew we were wrong to feel ashamed. The shame was growing inside me, churning in my guts, eating me from the inside, liquefying me on the spot. I wanted to reply but didn't have the courage to. Overwhelmed by accusatory eyes, I felt too young, too unjustified. Out of nowhere, I had a sudden urge: The shame had turned to liquid. I needed to be rid of it at all costs, to evacuate it, sloosh it down a urinal and on into the deep foul waters of a sewage treatment plant, mired in filth and forgotten, to fend off the terror of being condemned to burn at the stake of different accents.

We were foreigners, and in French, *foreigner* is the same word as *stranger*, which carries within it the word *strange*. So we were strange. Trying to disguise my discomfort, I took my sister's hand. I was scared to meet my mother's eye. I closed my eyes; I was going to get out of that store, away from this metatheater of our distress; I was going to walk through the store and open the door. And slam it? No, close it politely, to avoid disturbing anyone. I just wanted to go home and pee out my strangeness and forget.

Just then I felt another pair of eyes of me, and I spotted him: Kader. He too had witnessed the scene. He wasn't laughing. He scowled furiously at the yellow-eyed guy, then kept his eyes on me with a conspiratorial twinkle. He raised his thumb and slowly turned it down to mean that the guy was just a miserable loser. Kader was on my side this time. I was back in the foreign kids' club. We weren't so different now. I gave him a thumbs-up in reply.

I decided to wait for my mother outside with my sister. Through the window I could see her gesticulating toward the salesman, who'd lost interest in her. I begged her to come out, the yellow-eyes show was over.

And yet its repercussions were reverberating all through my body: *Yes, ma'am, I have yellow eyes, ma'am.*

Was I the only one who saw the invisible line marked out by this sarcasm? No one around us had supported us, no one had sympathized. Everyone's contemptuous intolerance of my mother's accent meant that we weren't allowed to react. The scoffing was way too much for me. It wasn't the first flash point I'd experienced, nor the first time I'd been a laughingstock, but you never get used to a situation like that, to so much misunderstanding over a few badly formulated words.

That humiliation left a bitter taste in our mouths all the way home. An open wound, and I can still feel the searing pain now. A little taunt tossed like a pebble into a pond, but it would send never-ending ripples over my whole life.

When we got home to my father, who was still sitting in his chair watching the TV news, he asked, "So, mine son, were you *courageuse* today?"

I didn't correct him.

Never again would I mention my father's grammatical mistakes, nor be annoyed by my mother's accent.

SCHISM

(Summer 1995)

I CAN'T explain why I no longer wanted to see your country, Dad. Adolescence may be a crisis, but it's also a schism, an evasion. I turned my back on Iraq and resented you for it.

In 1995, the grim year of the blockade, the country had changed. My mother, my sister, and I had seen the realities of sanctions firsthand: With the airport destroyed, international flights were canceled, and we set off for neighboring Jordan—twelve hours in a car across the desert. And in the middle of it, Trabil with its frontier and its unbearable destitution. Sanctions had Iraqis by the throat. The spectacular devaluation of the Iraqi dinar had increased prices fortyfold. A lead weight was bearing down on the country. Baghdad was badly affected. Fallujah was suffocating. Everyone was hungry. Everyone was angry. I was fifteen when I watched my cousins carry crates to the market instead of going to school, fifteen when my uncles showed me their war wounds, fifteen when I heard that Iraq was no longer allowed to import essential commodities, not even pencils. The country that invented writing was deprived of pencils... you couldn't make it up. I saw filthy hospitals with no beds, patients with no medication, doctors with no anesthetics. I went home to France sickened by a summer when too much horror had exploded right in my face.

The same scene played out every evening at nightfall: Children in rags, tormented by the heat and their thirst, descended on cars caught in traffic. There was no begging before the sanctions, I was told. These children refused to feel nostalgia for a time they hadn't known. Their future was blocked off, and now they trailed their poverty past cars whose occupants had stopped even looking at them.

Over the next few years, the Iraq of my childhood and my extended family drifted away from me, despite very occasional letters. My cousins lived their lives of sanctions, and from their modest words I discovered the misfortune of a whole people. The UN was wheeling and dealing with Saddam over "oil for food." The powerful elite was growing rich for all to see. The lower echelons in Iraq were shifting gears to anger. Anger that needed only the tiniest spark to detonate. Dignitaries from around the world were lining their pockets, and the abandoned Iraqi people had to suffer the consequences. The summer of 1995 ended in a climate of suspicion with everyone eyeing everyone else. Brothers spied on brothers, sisters on sisters. By retreating to its inner sanctum, the Iraqi regime had taken with it the vestiges of its population's dignity. And the country was dying along with its people.

As I grew up, I became like a medical student who refused to confront death. Iraq was dying, and I'd turned my back on it. I wanted to shrug off this deadweight in my identity, although I still couldn't suppress a familiar sense of imposture. Why was I born in France and not Iraq? Who would I have been over there? My father's exile had spared my sister and me the war with Iran, then the Gulf War and the injustices of the sanctions. I lived in peace when I should have been born in Fallujah and suffered bombings and shortages. In 1989 I'd had a head full of dreams, but when I returned to France after our 1995 visit to Iraq it was with a heavy heart and a mind saturated by too much horror.

———

We were broke, and, like Saddam's regime, my father shut himself away completely. That summer I realized that he'd given up once and for all. He was *too tired*, and his face grew grimmer and grimmer as Iraq descended into darkness. I couldn't bear it any longer. The Iraq I'd known in 1989 had vanished, and I refused to see this new version. I opted to break off all ties. I lived in France so I chose to close my eyes, get on with my schoolwork, and go out with my friends. Basically, make the most of life.

I wasn't robust enough to witness the destruction of a people every summer and then trot glibly back to France to enjoy my unfair privilege. I'd grasped the fact that, over there, the tiniest thing could bring happiness, whereas here everything made us sad. That's when I decided to stop eating dinner: to know what it felt like being hungry at bedtime and on waking, to be connected to what Iraqis were suffering—much to my parents' distress.

One evening when I was criticizing my father for the fact that I was born in France, he studied me for a long time and then, beside himself with rage, he overturned the table we were sitting at.

"You have no idea how lucky you are!"

We can be cruel as teenagers. We think we know it all, we don't want to listen, we don't want to understand, we make summary judgments, and we condemn without evidence.

"Oh, don't tell me, is it too complicated? Are you going to clam up again?"

I wanted to hurt him, to inflict all the angst of my childhood on him. I should never have known that faraway country that was sinking fast, it was his fault. All the misery had come too close for me to bear, and I spat it back out with my tears, throwing the blame on my father. Who was I, then, if he wouldn't talk to me, if I knew nothing about him? What sort of truth was I being protected from?

"So, you won't talk?"

"Get out! Forget Iraq! It's finished!" he roared in fury.

He was bound to be right. And I wanted to forget and to sink into the dark waters of our lost country with him.

For years to come I turned a blind eye to my father's emotional stress.

MAHDAWI CAFÉ

(Summer 1963)

RAMI WAS nineteen and his taciturn father had died a few months earlier, sitting with a pile of forms that needed filling out. The professional writer had become invaluable to Fallujah's inhabitants; he was one of the few educated people in town. Every last administrative document went through his hands. Everyone thought he was asleep that day, but his heart had stopped beating. A heart attack had claimed him.

Samiya had taken care of her husband's funeral arrangements. He'd expressed no wishes and she made the most of this to bury him far from Muhja, at the opposite end of the cemetery. Rami struggled to accept Samiya's behavior at the funeral: Her face had stayed dry of tears, a cold landscape devoid of emotion. Rami had just lost his father, and the town its scribe. With nothing and no one left to lose, he decided to leave Fallujah—and Samiya—for Baghdad.

It was five years since the revolution. In its honor, a triangular triumphal arch in Italian marble was erected opposite a new mosque built at the same time to avoid upsetting Baghdad's tribal heart. Rami found it hard to come to terms with the Soviet realism of the monument, as did all revolutionaries who—in spite of everything—still clung to tradition. Architects from other countries came and contributed to transforming the city to mark the fall of the monarchy. Beside the large Bab Al-Sharqi market a new open space was established: Liberation Square. Close to the nearby National Museum the Swiss built a modern central bank. And lastly, the wide imposing 14th of July Street was built. The overall effect was heightened by a final, more political touch: a series of paintings of soldiers, workmen, and agricultural workers united in a brotherly spirit of revolution; several huge likenesses of the leader "Abdel Karim"; and a proliferation of portraits of Marx, Engels, Lenin, and even Stalin. Communist propaganda and this personality cult were deployed all over the city with willful rigor and on a gigantic scale. Rami felt that Baghdad had grown less beautiful since July 14, 1958.

Rami and Hatem lived with two students in a small apartment in the Karrada neighborhood, right in the heart of the capital. Their evenings consisted of frugal meals between cash-strapped friends, washed down with arak, livened with green and black olives, and spiced with political debate. When they'd had a little too much to drink, they would all start singing—and Rami excelled at this in his spare time. As if he had some premonition, Rami sang about the absurdities of the revolution, its opponents in prison, and what would happen if he continued handing out leaflets on the street. And if he had to die for his beliefs, then it would inevitably be a fine death, as beautiful as the words that had lit up his dark life: *Thawra, Hurira, Ishitrakiya*—Revolution, Liberty, Socialism. As beautiful as the new word that had appeared in everyday speech: activism.

Activism now took up most of Rami's life. Since July 14, 1958, people could be openly activist in universities, on the streets, at cafés, and particularly at the Mahdawi Café. Before becoming Baghdad's most popular café, the huge typically Iraqi brick-and-plaster building had already been a local institution during the monarchy, a sports club for the elite. Here Rami and Hatem found an unhoped-for venue where social class had disappeared, at least to all appearances. Most discussion groups stayed faithful to the Communist ideal put forward by General Qasim. Some intoned hymns to its glory, intoxicating almost the whole, smoke-filled room, which was mostly due to collective hypnosis and a sort of proletarian mysticism. In among them, waiters holding their metal trays above shoulder height came and went in a skillful choreography to bring customers glasses filled to the brim with tea. This club, which was the preserve of the democratic youth, was where debate met conspiracy, where the country's history could be made and undone over a glass of tea.

The Mahdawi became the nerve center for the new republic's dissenters. It was full during the day, and the manager opened all the windows and the big door out onto the street. Books and newspapers were provided for customers. And a new rule was now posted by the café's entrance: *No dominoes or other games here. People come here to read and talk.* By contrast, at night, a different type of activist used a more discreet entrance at the back of the small room, and they were known as "the last customers." They arrived toward the end of the evening and left at dawn. They were the most radical and their motto was: "The last shall be first." These regulars would arrive carrying books, which they set down on the tea- and sugar-spattered tables, and they would leave with a pistol in their belts. The Mahdawi might officially close at midnight, but it had two lives. Rami and Hatem were part of its second life, with these "last customers."

There were three opposing political currents in Iraq at the time: Communism, whose members were loyal to Qasim; the Baath Party, a growing Arab nationalist movement; and Trotskyism, to which Rami adhered. Drawn to far-left circles, he'd devoured biographies of the major players in the Bolshevik Revolution, then set his sights on Lev Davidovich Bronstein, alias Leon Trotsky, a hero of the October Revolution and founder of the Red Army. Everything about the man—his nomadic life and his iron fist as much as his political intelligence—thrilled Rami. And he'd taken to announcing to anyone who would listen: "Trotsky released me from my mental prison and put me to the test of real life."

———

One evening, Rami found Hatem involved in a heated discussion with some other activists. Hatem was clearly irritated by these men in their made-to-measure suits who drove German cars and continued their clandestine meetings at the café in fancy houses around the capital. Rami was wary of them and hesitated to join in their discussions. Hatem could talk of nothing but revolution. It was true, that this political emulation was spreading through all parts of Iraqi society, but the men in conversation with Hatem were Baath militants, dangerous patriots. And the Baath Party was casting its web over Baghdad. Its members, who were especially violent, were cunning strategists.

The revolution wouldn't last, Rami was sure of it. A fault line had been opened up and plotters would soon be streaming in through it. This thought alone was enough to make him shudder. There may still have been feverish revolutionary spirit at the Mahdawi, but there was already a mood of counterrevolution in the air. Only those who spoke the least would survive, Rami thought, because the most insignificant pronouncement could be interpreted as a sign of rebellion against the powers that be. In among the raised fists and fevered brows, young men in ties were taking up a defiant stance.

It was dark outside and the diffuse light inside the café tempered forbidden conversations. For the rest of his life Rami would remember that evening when a slim man with a barrel chest thumped his fist on a table amid the general euphoria and cast an icy eye around the room. This man, who was known for his relentless persecution of Communists, was a militant nationalist climbing his way up the Baath Party's ranks thanks to a series of violent acts. The dozen or so men in black suits who were with him stood behind him in a semicircle. Proudly flaunting the gun in his belt, the man rose to his feet and pointed at the group that included Rami and Hatem.

"Arabs will never accept Communism in their country," he said. "We despise the Soviets, and you'll pay for it someday."

Then he left the premises just as he'd arrived, furtively, without a backward glance, leaving everyone stunned by his threats. In the short ensuing silence, Rami was gripped by an obscure feeling of horror. It had taken him a while to recognize this man who'd turned to look at him.

It was Saad. Samiya's son had joined the Baath Party, the enemy. Rami may have run away but Saad, and therefore Samiya, had caught up with him.

THE LOST REVOLUTION

(Summer 1968)

FIVE YEARS had passed, and Rami's fears were being confirmed: There had been a succession of coups and the republic had descended into the cesspool of dictatorship. First came a coup orchestrated by another general, new slogans abounded, then democratic debate was challenged by a new lexicon. Words such as *security, patriotism,* and *purge* now reverberated around the streets of Baghdad.

And then things accelerated.

General Abd al-Karim Qasim was killed live on television in 1963. At the hand of his longtime ally General Abdul Salam Arif, even though this assassin had been in the front lines of the attack on Baghdad's royal palace on July 14, 1958. With the support of the Baath Party, he'd organized a coup against Qasim on February 8, 1963, and immediately had him executed. The National Council elected Abdul Salam Arif as president of the republic when the Baath Party had in fact taken power and was tracking its opponents who had been involved in the coup, as well as all Communists—including Rami and Hatem.

This brutal repression was headed up by a man called Saddam Hussein, one of the Baath leaders who'd emerged from the shadows into the light.

———

Military service had been extended so Rami and Hatem were mobilized. This proved a real boon for them, offering them an escape from the climate of tyranny. They could turn away from Baghdad and switch to southern Iraq, sheltered from the hunt for dissidents.

In Basra, dressed in their army uniforms, Rami and Hatem were just ordinary soldiers with nothing to defend or attack. Their days filed by, one much like the other. Their clothes were not at all adapted to the Iraqi climate, having been designed for Soviet soldiers to withstand the cold—palming them off on the Iraqi army as a gift could actually be seen as a bad joke.

One day their unit was mobilized to Shaibah Air Base to greet two delegations, one Egyptian and one Soviet, along with ministers from these countries. On the runway, Rami, Hatem, and dozens of other soldiers—all of them stuffed into their overly thick jackets—waited many long hours under a scorching sun. The officials in the Soviet delegation were coming to conclude the sale of L-29s and MiG-21s to Iraq, which would then be free of American imperialism—a process with which the Egyptians wanted to be associated. And the delegations had been invited to watch a demonstration by Iraqi pilots.

Apart from the red brick walls, there was not much left of this former British air base. The legend goes that Her Majesty's forces had built it here because they could smell the food being cooked in the village of Shaibah—particularly the local specialty, masgouf, which was eaten every Wednesday.

The two friends who'd had so many glorious illusions about revolution were becoming disillusioned. They weren't interested in being recruits at the academy because they didn't want to make this their career. During their enforced evenings off, Rami and Hatem usually joined friends in their apartments to drink arak, play poker, and eat food they'd all prepared. They each contributed something, giving their lackluster days a semblance of solidarity and friendliness. Once the Soviet, Iraqi, and Egyptian ministers had signed their contract and left with promises of a pact of friendship and security in the face of American imperialism, the day ended in the usual way.

Crushed by the heat, Rami and Hatem stared straight ahead to the Shatt al-Arab, where the Tigris and the Euphrates became one. The sinking sun made the water glint orange. The thermometer had skimmed close to 122 degrees that day. Hatem had fallen asleep on his right side under some date palms along the left bank in Basra, the Venice of the Middle East. A brief respite after the one significant event of the day, which had passed off without incident. Rami took a drag on his cigarette as he remembered the Euphrates and the watermelons, and his near drowning. The memory had never faded and popped up from time to time like a lingering threat of submersion on time delay. And since then, claustrophobia had come into his life: He could no longer bear confined spaces and felt stifled by the mere thought of a locked door.

"It's fucking boring doing nothing, right?" Hatem grumbled.

The riverbanks were accumulating mist in the heat and the men were almost anesthetized. Hatem went on snoozing and Rami, lying with his hands behind his neck, had to fight to stay awake.

A few minutes later, Rami heard Hatem's voice in the distance.

"Get up, Rami, we're going."

"Where to?"

"You'll see."

Hatem led Rami through unfamiliar, labyrinthine little streets. They were surrounded by houses with palm-leaf roofs, and people living frugally from buffalo farming, fishing, and gathering bulrushes. A narrow passageway brought them to a deserted blind alley with a single house at the far end. Hatem responded to each of his friend's hesitations and questions with, "It's a surprise. Follow me."

When they reached the house, which reminded Rami of his childhood home, Hatem knocked three times at the metal gate. The gate opened to reveal a sleepy, gray face. Then a smile widened, showing damaged teeth. The man gestured for them to come in with a polite *Tafadhali*, and he pointed toward a wooden door.

Inside, three men were sitting on a Persian carpet. Not one of them spoke and they too were in uniform. Rami sat down cautiously, greeting them with a little wave and secretly hoping the door wouldn't be locked. Like a couple of children, he and Hatem sat against the cool walls of this small brick house, and the hot sugary cardamom tea that they were served warmed the rather sinister atmosphere in the room, which was brightened only by floral plastic curtains.

A few minutes later, an old woman wearing a black abaya and an impenetrable expression came into the room. She sat down and mumbled a few verses before gesturing for Rami to come closer to her. Perplexed, he glanced at Hatem, who nodded with a twinkle of amusement in his eyes, and the other three men watched approvingly.

The old woman lit an oil lamp and the flame danced at her feet. Without paying any attention to Rami, she took a metal rod from an inside pocket and put it into the flame. After a few seconds, she ran the rod over her tongue several times, making small jerking movements as if to avoid burning herself. Rami winced but the seer didn't appear to notice. He thought the ceremony strange and wondered what the hell he was doing there. The woman was now studying her copper rod in minute detail. She said nothing for a while, then finally looked up at Rami, before sending him back to sit next to Hatem, who was still amused by his friend's discomfort.

The woman then called them into another room one after the other. Of the three men who went through before Rami and Hatem, two returned with expressionless faces, while the third came out smiling.

"Rami Ahmed!"

Rami stood up carefully so as not to spill his tea and followed the woman to the far end of a dark room furnished with just two plastic chairs and a table on which the mysterious copper rod lay. The woman took Rami's hand firmly and started talking. She was so strong that Rami couldn't free himself from her clutches. When he looked at her, he couldn't suppress a yelp. Impossible, no, it was impossible. The old woman was his stepmother, Samiya. She was crushing his hand and he couldn't move. Her powerful hand had trapped his like a pair of pincers. Rami had no choice but to listen to what she had to tell him.

"There will be four major incidents in your life. The first has already happened. The second will happen this year. The last two will come one after the other in the same year, in another country, when you're a mature man," she whispered, her eyes pinned on the copper rod. "In the first, I see a river where you nearly drowned. You managed to get out. A close friend saved you just in time. In the second, I can see you locked in somewhere, surrounded by high-ranking men, you'll be in a very difficult situation. You'll be very frightened. But you will also manage to get out. In the third ordeal, I see a blue sky. I can see the vast expanses of the desert. You'll manage to get out of the situation in your own way yet again. In the fourth event, I can see a white room."

The seer paused for a while and Rami noticed something in her face for the first time—a combination of concern and embarrassment.

Out of nowhere there was a clap of thunder, and Rami woke with a scream to see Hatem leaning over him with his fists on his hips.

"You were having a horrible nightmare, my little lizard. What was it about?"

"Was I asleep for long? I thought you were the one sleeping."

"You slept for a century."

The fierce blue of the sky, the occasional wispy cloud... Rami lay with his arms by his sides and took a big deep breath. The dream—or nightmare—had felt so real. His amazement at Samiya's predictions was followed by profound anxiety. The first accident certainly had happened. In the Euphrates. And he'd gotten out. But what did the *white room* mean? And, if his dream was telling the truth, what did the future have in store for him?

A few months later, Rami had completely forgotten Samiya's predictions. Life carried on. In exchange for a fee, Rami and Hatem were released from their obligation to national service for the same reason as everyone who put their hand in their pocket: responsibility for dependents who would not have adequate resources if the young soldier was enlisted.

The friends returned to Baghdad and their clandestine political leanings. Rami was offered a civil servant position at the Ministry of Youth, acting as a guide for foreign delegations who were flocking to Iraq. It was the perfect job for Rami, who could pursue his militant tendencies. The first delegation he welcomed was French, activists from the far-left Lutte Ouvrière party. He didn't know it yet but this would be a determining moment for him.

Ten years had passed since the revolution. The triangular triumphal arch still stood; Bab Al-Sharqi was still called Liberation Square and was still dominated by its colossal bronze statue built by the Soviets. Almost everywhere, portraits of General Qasim had been replaced with ones of Saddam Hussein and his uncle, President Hassan al-Bakr. As for the likenesses of Marx, Lenin, Stalin, and Khrushchev, they had disappeared.

The Baath Party, and it alone, was now in power—the sole, soul-destroying party.

THE LAST PALACE

(Spring 1971)

UNDER SADDAM Hussein's influence, Iraq was gradually becoming an authoritarian state. People had grown paranoid, with everyone spying on everyone else. Police officers were under surveillance, and so were intelligence officers, monitored by counterespionage agents. The regime's security arrangements were descending into obsession.

From the early 1970s, at least three organizations—the Republican Guard, the Special Forces, and the Popular Mobilization Forces—were detailed to hunt down all opponents of the regime. And even these three institutions spied on one another. Thanks to Saddam Hussein's strategy of fear, which stated that every citizen must be the eyes and ears of the state or risk being the target of repression, the denunciation process worked well. And a succession of executions—of traitors, spies, and other rebels—were carried out to terrify the population.

In 1971, the Communist Party and the Baath Party entered into an agreement against their common enemies, the Trotskyites, of which Rami was one. While he worked as a guide for the ministry, he still handed out leaflets, debated at discreet, pop-up conferences, and shouted down nationalist tendencies. Until dawn on April 24, 1971.

At four in the morning, when the black of the sky was giving way to mauve and the chaos on Al Rashid Street had calmed, "dawn visitors" entered Rami's home without knocking. This was what Saddam Hussein's henchmen were called. Firmly and without using violence, the four "visitors" ordered Rami to follow them without a struggle. In very few words. Their reputation gave them authority. They knew everything: his ideas, his commitment, whom he saw, even down to what time of day he distributed leaflets. But also, meetings in which he'd participated. One of the men pulled a black knit cap over Rami's face to cover his eyes.

Less than an hour later, after they'd passed a final checkpoint, the cap was removed. Nothing but darkness and silence around him. The car drove on for a few minutes before stopping again. The cap was put back over his head. Rami just had time to see an imposing building surrounded by water. The place looks like a closely guarded castle, he thought to himself. The men led him out of the car without using insults or brutality; their movements were controlled, almost mechanical, with a gentleness that belied the gravity of the situation.

"Welcome to the last palace," one of them whispered.

Did Rami know that the last palace had been the residence of King Faisal, who was shot by Abd al-Karim Qasim's forces during a coup in July 1958? That it had been a symbol of decadence until it was turned into a prison? That countless dissidents were rotting here? That its nickname was based on the rumor that no one came out of here alive?

The commando unit surrounded Rami. He could hear their footsteps in what must have been a long corridor. They went down a winding staircase that seemed to descend into an abyss. Rami could feel his heart constricting at the thought of never seeing the light of day again. Strangely, he found himself hoping he would end up in a windowless cell. What prospects could windows possibly offer him if not of hell? One of the dawn visitors opened the last door behind which there lingered an acidic, ferrous stench, the smell of blood and fear. At this point, Rami thought dying wouldn't be such a big deal. But the route to it would be the terrible part. He'd heard talk of instruments of torture inherited from the Nazis. Was the human race still capable of such horrors? he wondered.

Welcome to the last palace. The words went round and round inside his head.

———

At the time, Rami was just a young activist, a kid from Fallujah handing out leaflets that called people to fight for the poorest of the poor. What did they hope to get from him?

The first torturer came into the cell in a fury. He grabbed Rami by the collar and dragged him into the seat of suffering. Strange objects were laid out on a table: spiked handcuffs, pliers, both large and small, a chair whose back-rest was angled forward so that whoever sat on it was bent double.

The man told Rami to put the handcuffs on himself, then asked, "Where's Hatem?"

Rami didn't reply.

"Where's Hatem?" the jailer asked again.

With each silence, he slapped Rami and tightened the handcuffs slightly.

"Names! We want names!"

Rami continued to say nothing about Hatem. He even claimed not to know him. Without tears or screams, he let the man batter him and stayed silent. His torturer left him alone all night, naked in the middle of the room, attached to the chair, his wrists bleeding. Would he ever recover the use of his hands?

The following day, he woke surrounded by four men, in a different room with an imposing desk in the middle of it. His boxes of books and his leaflets had been spread out on the floor. The men circled around him. All at once, Rami started to smile, then to laugh. Perhaps he was going mad? The more he laughed, the more the men beat him. His head was flung from left to right, his body slammed against the walls. The light in the room danced before his eyes.

Night and day for three months he was asked the same question, delivered with the same physical abuse.

"Where's Hatem?"

"I don't know."

"It's in your interest to confess."

"Confess what?"

"Look at this photo. That's you, isn't it? And that there is Hatem, can you see?"

Rami could make out a table at the back of the Mahdawi Café. Still, he didn't say anything.

"You don't want to talk, so we'll keep going. You'll own up eventually, you'll see."

Own up. Gradually, the thought that he would never leave this prison crept over Rami. The thought that it was a new world, and he needed to adapt to it and live, despite the daily suffering and death hanging over him. Agreeing to be reduced by turns to the status of circus animal or one sent for slaughter.

On the very first day his head was shaved. Every morning he was sprayed with ice-cold water in his tiny cell. Prisoners had to walk with their hands behind their back, heads lowered, alert, ready for every order given by their jailers.

These evils were his daily existence.

Torture. Moans.

Day. Night.

Torture. Gasps.

Night. Night. Day.

Torture. Night.

An endless cycle of madness and eroding reason.

Sometimes Rami would wake on the ground, unable to establish how long he'd been unconscious. When alone, he allowed himself a few tears. Under torture, he howled till he was hoarse. But he withstood it. Rami discovered that he had a resistance to suffering he'd never suspected. His country was far more important than he was, and he was stronger than this prison, than slamming doors and screams in the night and the mortal silence that followed. All these sounds became imprinted on his mind. He would never be rid of them.

But what of the other voice, on the night of his arrest? The one whose despotic inflection came back to him day after day, tormenting him to the point of insanity.

Welcome to the last palace. The voice he just couldn't forget, it felt so familiar, bringing old memories to the surface. Was it possible? Was it Saad's voice? The last time Rami had seen him, the whole of the Mahdawi Café had quaked at the threats for which Rami was now clearly suffering the consequences. This is all just a nightmare, I'll wake up soon, Rami thought.

All of a sudden, a nasal voice replaced the one he recognized from his childhood.

"Get up, you filthy dogs!"

Hauled from their cells, the detainees were herded with beating sticks to the middle of a floodlit yard. Standing in a long line of prisoners, Rami skulked like all the others.

"It's Thursday," came the grating, fake cheerful voice of a faceless officer. "Theater time!"

Theater. A display up on a platform, designed to humiliate the most important detainees. They were asked to play the clown or perform impossible physical feats with violent reprisals as a special bonus if they failed. The jailers focused their attentions on officers, high-ranking officials, ministers, and anyone who had plotted against the regime. None of them would ever get out. They would die one way or another: by torture, by humiliation, or by suicide. For the others, physical abuse was already ingrained in their skin; whereas mental torture imprinted itself over time. It couldn't be forgotten. It would be with them their whole lives. In Iraq, it was better to die than be humiliated in public. This "theater" was an opportunity to see who was being held there, and Rami found himself looking for Hatem, but he couldn't see him anywhere.

Rami's limbs were stiff and numb, his mouth dry, his throat constricted, and he couldn't believe what he was witnessing. Some of the guards came over to the prisoners and selected a man who had clearly been pitifully weakened by torture. He fell to the ground and the jailers yanked him by his arms, almost pulling them from their sockets. In front of the twenty or so watching detainees, they kept trying to force him to his feet. The man was an activist accused of plotting, and Rami knew him. He had been this man's pupil. And his victim. This was the man who had accused Rami of cheating, his math teacher, Mr. Fadil. He had been chosen to be the clown for that evening's performance.

It seemed a simple enough challenge. A metal bar—probably used for beating prisoners—was held at shoulder height between two guards. A bottle of water was put onto Fadil's head, and he had to walk under the bar without toppling the bottle. In anticipation, the other prisoners were asked to liven things up with cheering and clapping to celebrate this theatrical event in a grim prison yard at the last palace.

Mr. Fadil stepped forward, rallied by the forced cheers from his frightened audience. He looked determined to get through this ambush. Every step mattered, every one was a victory. Rami admired his self-assurance. He saw his teacher as he'd appeared during the revolution, a militant intoxicated by the hope of change. It took poise and courage, or perhaps despair, to implement what had been asked of him in the face of threats from his unsmiling, mustached tormentors. He was close to succeeding when one of the guards tripped him at the last minute, to enforced laughter from the onlookers. The prisoner got back to his feet. The whooping stopped abruptly and a strange silence settled over the scene. Fadil caught Rami's eye, a moment Rami would never forget. Then the jailers pulled Fadil by his collar and he let himself be led away with no resistance. The door closed behind them. The show was over.

Rami never heard mention of Fadil again.

POLICE CUSTODY

(Summer 1998)

IMPRISONMENT DIDN'T conjure many feelings in me. I'd never experienced it. But if I dig through my memory, I think that, just for a few hours, I had a taste of what my father endured for three months—with no comparison in terms of torture, of course. The only memory I can dig up from this time is the stupid idea that unintentionally brought me closer to my father.

Water had flowed under the bridge and our disagreements had been dissolved by life. As a teenager, when I'd lost sight of my home country, the world felt too dark, too unfair, and too cold a place. So my father and I avoided talking about Iraq or any topic likely to cause tension. We lived under the same roof without really communicating. He buried himself deeper into his apolitical asylum, and I into my ostracized neighborhood.

The stupid idea came from Kader, who'd now taken to me. I was no longer the odd one out; I'd become the Iraqi.

He'd left high school, while I was still studying without knowing where that might lead. I didn't think much about my future. Kader and I found foolish, underhand, discreet ways of earning money in our neighborhood, unable to avoid the lure of street life and its collateral damage.

On the day in question, we were both feeling very low. A local guy called Lazar had been stabbed in the gut the day before. Not stabbed just to scare him, or stabbed in legitimate self-defense, but stabbed to kill. The blade slicing upward. A technique systematically defined as premeditated murder and that leads straight to court. I passed out when I saw Lazar lying on his hospital bed, unable to eat, contorted in pain, and fruitlessly pressing on the button for more morphine. When I came to, I also realized I could never be a doctor. Luckily, Lazar survived. He was an ordinary guy who hadn't gone looking for trouble. He'd been on his way home when a man had appeared out of nowhere screaming revenge in the name of a law that held sway in the neighborhood: an eye for an eye. Lazar had been made to pay for some previous event about which we knew nothing.

Everyone wanted to do something, retaliate, yell, break stuff. And because boredom is a bad adviser, Kader then came up with his lousy idea: We didn't have it in us to kill anyone, so we would scare the neighboring district.

"Let's go find the motherfucker," Kader suggested.

I followed my closest friends, Kader and Franck, unsure of what I was doing or why. I wanted to become one of the guys people were afraid of, something I wasn't at the

time and never would be; I wanted to read my own fear in
the eyes of people who would see me as a serious gangster.
I hadn't completely addressed the problem that faces all
teenagers—the question of choice. What did I want to be?
As teenagers we may well have adult bodies but the child
in us doesn't always have the courage to say no. Yes, I'd
sometimes had that courage, or at least the intention had
been there. And then I backtracked every time, I came back
to the same old me, I recognized these future versions of
myself as clones that I didn't want to be or to become. But
Lazar had nearly died, and we had to respond.

Kader took us to the flea market in Clignancourt, where
you could buy fake guns. We were determined to find the
attacker and make him pay for tarnishing Lazar's innocence.
I emerged from the armory with something that looked exactly like the revolver my uncle Saad had let me carry.

It was a swelteringly hot day with humidity levels to
curl the straightest of hair. Saint-Lazare station. Passengers
on the train turned to watch us as we walked through the
carriages looking for an empty one. We eventually decided
to hole up on the upper deck of a carriage in the middle of
the train.

The idea was to slink unnoticed into the neighborhood.
I took the gun from my bag, to approving glances from my
accomplices. I just wanted to look at it. It was like something straight out of an American cop show, or Fallujah. It
was all very well being alone in the carriage, but everyone
could see us through the windows—three teenagers playing with a gun. We were so busy examining the thing we

didn't notice that the train was taking a long time to leave. I only registered when four plainclothes police officers took aim at me with a pistol. A very real one.

"Drop your weapon!" one of them yelled in a voice as caricatured as those proverbial television series.

I thought I was going to die there and then. I put the toy down on the leather seat and raised my hands. Passengers on the platform and in the next carriage looked relieved and eyed me scornfully. Without realizing it, we'd terrorized a whole train and part of the station.

When I told the officers that the pistol was fake, one of them retorted, "Well, you're going to have a taste of *real* police custody, then you won't feel so smart."

"What an asshole! The kid's a total pea brain," added one of his fellow officers.

So, the day before I turned eighteen, I ended up cuffed and being led away by four cops, heading for Saint-Lazare station police precinct while onlookers gawped.

––––––––––

In an office at the precinct, I was asked my family name, first name, birth date, address, and phone number, then I was cuffed to a radiator.

"Say, this one's still a minor!" said one of the men, sitting at a computer, laughing. "But not for long, guys." He looked at me. "We'll have to call your parents."

I explained that my parents lived a long way away, asked if they could wait till I became an adult, it would only be a few hours, then I could sign the statement myself. He didn't want to listen and seemed amused by the situation.

"I tell you what, let's call them right now."

He dialed the number, keeping one snickering eye on me.

"Yes, good evening, could I speak to the father of one Euphrates Ahmed?...Yes, Saint-Lazare station, that's right...Don't worry, we're keeping him warm for you..."

He hung up with a sneer.

"There you are! All set for a birthday at the precinct, you can wait in the cells. A little spell in custody is our gift."

And so I was put in custody for possession of a category C weapon: "An object that could constitute a weapon that is a threat to public safety." A poet who'd temporarily occupied the cell had engraved these words on the wall: *The world won't budge, the judges judge, and the law makes the law.* Being locked in a cell taught me something—I was claustrophobic.

Although only a hair's breadth from majority, I was not yet responsible for my own life, I was subject to my father's law. Sitting on that small stone bench with that dirty blanket and that locked door, I felt naked. I'd already been asked to remove my belt and shoelaces. The door had been locked to humiliate me. I could hear police officers in the corridor laughing about me as they checked my identity. It was about eleven in the evening.

"Happy birthday, pea brain," one of them jeered.

An officer started whistling "Happy Birthday," others clapped, and soon the whole corridor was celebrating my birthday. I laughed along grudgingly until I hit eighteen.

A few hours later, my father came to collect me from the precinct. I was an adult. I felt stupid. He came up to me slowly, looking calm, a far cry from the anger I thought I would have provoked.

"It's just as well, my son," he said gently.

Surprised, I looked at him questioningly.

"It's just as well you've experienced this. Now you know how it feels to be locked in a cell, even just for a few hours. That's how you learn to be a man. Part of the initiation process involves stooping very low. What do you think learning means? It means messing around a bit, letting go of old ideas in favor of new ones, seeing bullshit from the inside, and then moving on. So, the way I see it, if you decide to stop your bullshit, that means you've decided to be a man. Bullshit's contagious, but it's not a virus, there's no vaccine for it."

I whistled. "Did you prepare that speech?"

"Of course I did, mine son!" He smiled.

Now we were two men on their way home.

"By the way, did you know they sang 'Happy Birthday' for me at the precinct?"

"No!"

"I swear it, the place is nuts."

We joked for the rest of the journey, even laughing till we cried. My rite of passage to adulthood hadn't gone as I'd anticipated. But reestablishing lines of communication with my father was the best of presents, inexpressible happiness, the last I remember.

ROOM 219

(September 5, 2019)

DID MY father notice the time passing after he reached his seventy-fifth summer? He came to Paris in 1972 at the age of twenty-nine, and a few decades later—*in the blink of an eye*, to quote my history teacher—here he was shut away in room 219, an amnesiac seventy-something.

He took a cigarette from his packet. As I watched him strike the match, I remembered the strange litany from my childhood, something he would recite whenever he was drunk. Over many years he would come out with this sentence with the same words and the same intonation: "And we will cross the bridge. And we will ambush them. And we will drive them out of the country!"

It wasn't about the bridge in Fallujah, I was sure of that. The incantation was a threat of violence and referred to enemies. When I asked him about it, he would say, "It's nothing, mine son, it's nothing." Other times, he'd say, "I have a secret I can't discuss. A secret that will die with me."

———

My father had his head in his hands. He pulled the oxygen tube from his nostrils and wiped his eyes with a handkerchief. I sat on the edge of the bed, not sure whether to comfort him or give him space.

"Why are you crying?" I asked.

"I don't know."

We were sticking to our mutual reserve; I felt more comfortable changing the subject.

"Dad, do you remember your Samsonite briefcase?"

He looked up, as if thinking. "Remember what?"

"Your briefcase that I found in the closet."

"My briefcase…"

"Does it ring any bells?"

"Yes, I think so."

Thirty years earlier, I'd found the card with the unfamiliar name on it in the briefcase with the combination lock.

As a child I knew nothing about my father's life, but I often attributed his sadness to that card. I've never been able to locate the seat of his pain. Since he lost his memory, I've felt as if I've been mending this broken father, giving him back his own story by trying not to prod where it hurts.

My father interrupted these thoughts by asking, "Can you tell me if the other guy made a success of his life?"

The other guy.

The one in the mirror. My father as he was before.

I was back in the room, with the two of us; him with his weary voice and me with drums pounding in my head.

I struggled to breathe. He had the same melancholy, far-away look as the father I'd once known. Before losing his memory, my father had been obsessed with failure. When he was angry, he often said he'd failed in life. So, for just a moment, it seemed I'd found him again. I gauged how much of his pessimism had bled into my personality: I always thought I'd failed at all the important things, picked the dud option with every decision, constantly ended up on the wrong side of success, and felt like an imposter if I ever came close to success because I reckoned it was meant for other people. Had he been successful? How could I answer a question like that? Where, when, and how did you set the bar for success?

The sky cracked open, and the white room darkened to gray. I leaned on the windowsill, watching raindrops spatter onto the panes. I wiped away the condensation and saw a few solitary patients trying to make it to shelter with the very thing that was killing them. Some of them were still smoking even though they were there to be cured of the effects of that toxin. It seemed absurd. My father had been poisoning himself for more than sixty years by smoking. I thought about his life before he lost his memory and the years when we avoided conversation, the years when we let silence do the talking. Until the doctor's prognosis. This pact of silence had been replaced by shared experiences with my father that I cherished.

Then I thought about that closet from my childhood again, about the reek of naphthalene and the smell in the briefcase with the combination lock. Where did that case go?

OUBLIETTE

(September 6, 2019)

WHEN I returned to my mother, she was ragged with anxiety, at home in the apartment that had been amputated of her husband, disoriented by my comings and goings to the clinic. Since my father's amnesia she seemed detached from the world, and no longer met up with neighbors—neither the Palestinian woman who was nostalgic about Saddam Hussein's regime, nor the Iraqi one content with today's Iraq. My mother has lived every moment of her time in France to the rhythm of Rami's breathing. Everything had become a means of keeping herself busy. Even when the place was spotless, she would dust the furniture, clean the fridge, and change the layout of the living room. Between two of her household chores, I quizzed her about the oubliette—that was what my father called the room in question. This housing-project apartment designed for large families had three bedrooms, one of which was tiny, and we used it as a storeroom.

———

When my sister and I left home, the room was first converted into a library, then my parents put an armchair in there for reading and a sofa bed. In fact, my father used the room for his daily siesta or to get away and be forgotten after a fight. It was his little sanctuary, a place where, he claimed, he could take off his glasses and leave them at the door, the perfect refuge to forget his problems and anything *complicated*—hence an oubliette. But he never guessed for a moment that one day he really would forget things.

I once pointed out that oubliettes were dungeons where people were locked away for all eternity to be forgotten, and he replied mischievously, "Don't worry, your mother never forgets to come wake me, and that doesn't mean I'm freed!"

The room was sacred. Since my father's illness, my mother had locked it. Before going in, I washed my hands and tidied my hair out of respect for it. I slipped the key into the lock and smiled at the creak of the handle, which used to indicate the end of nap time. I took a deep breath and, as if entering a library, I stepped into that room where my father used to retreat for some peace and quiet. I closed the door behind me so I could be alone with the things in there. It all looked desperately listless. The bookcase, the reading chair, the bed for his siestas—everything was frozen in time as if my father had left in a hurry. The imprint of his body was still clear on the mattress. A whole lifetime's worth of books were lined up on a shelf: Marx's *Capital, Iraq: Contradictions and Development*, and farther on *The Betrayed Revolution*. There were photos too. Him with my mother in Egypt, on the banks of the Nile. The two of them smiling at Petra in Jordan.

"We're not supposed to take photos of life's sad times," he once told me. "That's why everyone smiles in photos."

Being in the oubliette without my father rekindled my sense of loss. I could close my eyes as much as I liked, he was everywhere. I had to accept the fact that the father I had once known was no longer there. He'd turned on his heel and capitulated, a prisoner of room 219. Would he ever come back? I could only glimpse details of him here, his stooped back, his amazing yawns, how he cleaned his glasses as if polishing precious metal, and the way he nodded at TV commercials whose secret meaning he alone had grasped, the evil subliminal message behind any new household product. A peculiar feeling of déjà vu.

I'd known this room full of life, but now nothing was more alive than his absence. Gone were the regular siestas—at around two in the afternoon—that he announced in half-spoken words as he tottered off, removing his glasses as if turning out one last light. I wasn't hoping to find revelations or obscure clues, I wanted to find words he'd written and to see that card again. That card seemed so unreal, something from another time, and I wanted to hold it in my hand again. I walked slowly around the room. What I was looking for fitted into a small case, and that was something I *would* be able to see, a dark brown Samsonite with a combination lock. 7 5 8. I now saw everything in a different light: 7 5 8 meant July 1958, my father's revolution. This was no coincidence. As I child, I'd hoped to find the truth. What I'd found was a lie.

Wasn't that precisely what I was doing with my father? Conjuring a feeling of déjà vu to stir up memories? A fascinating exercise, but dangerous too because—however well-intentioned—didn't I run the risk of distorting his memory and lying? I stopped in front of that closet from my childhood. A white closet that had once looked huge to me, so imposing that it alone appeared to hold up the ceiling. It had seemed like a world of wonders waiting to be explored.

I opened both doors and was assailed by a blast of naphthalene, a smell that, as a child, I identified with closets and suitcases, and that I started to love the day I found my father's briefcase. A travel-related smell that had followed me all the way to Iraq. The fragrance of difficult departures and painful goodbyes when I left Fallujah for Baghdad; of border checks in Jordan and then Iraq on the frontier at Trabil; and of the last tears hidden behind masculine reserve. Those mothballs made my heart constrict. Olfactory memory is treacherous and oversimplified.

Inside the case I found two ten-franc bills. On the first was Hector Berlioz, baton in hand with his orchestra behind him. On the other was Voltaire wearing his wig and holding a pen. How many people had handled those bills? From the large inside pocket, I took a red, white, and blue folder with an image on the front of Marianne brandishing the French flag. Written along the bottom was the motto of the French Republic: Liberty, Equality, Fraternity. In the very depths of the pocket was a set of black and gray prayer beads. These objects now lined up together like the links in a chain, the different stages in a life.

It was all in that briefcase.

Since my father's amnesia, I've often questioned my own memory. What was it that I really told Rami?

I found the photo of my father as a young man again. Studying it more closely, I realized that—contrary to my recollection—he looked sad. The picture of happiness seen through my child's eyes had evaporated. Among some newspaper cuttings, I came across the card with the false name on it. I slipped it into my billfold. And I cast my mind back to Iraq and the year when war struck us again.

THE INVASION

(Spring 2003)

ON THE night of March 19, 2003, everything came tumbling down.

We were all glued to the television at home. George W. Bush's ultimatum had just expired and every news channel in the world was tuned to Baghdad. We waited in silence, anticipating the first bomb blast, the slightest flash of light in the skies over the Iraqi capital. My parents had been worrying for a few weeks already. It was difficult to contemplate the post-Saddam question—it struck them as impossible: The dictator couldn't be deposed after so many decades of terror. And even though my father had been a victim of the rais, he was against this invasion; he sensed the political stakes couched within the American lie.

When the first missiles fell from the sky, I couldn't bear to watch the televised massacre orchestrated by the injustice of this world. The same green sky as in 1991, the same fireworks that had made my father, in his drunken state, weep for his lacerated country. The different angle, the enigmatic words. I couldn't take any more. I went out for some air and dived into a Métro station as if that might obliterate everything. I thought about my extended family, all the people I'd come to know in Iraq. What was left of my country? Of my childhood memories? And my teenage turmoil?

Sully-Morland station.

A woman stepped onto the subway, holding a mic in one hand and pulling along a speaker with the other. We were the only two passengers, but she sat opposite me and said a few words before starting to sing.

"This song is in homage to the women and children of Iraq who are living and dying under bombs tonight. Freedom. Freedom to the Iraqi people."

She looked me right in the eye—it was extraordinary. I was wandering around in the subway to get away from the bombing in Iraq and it had come looking for me, as if by magic. The song was about freedom and starry skies.

It was eleven in the evening in France, one in the morning in Iraq, and Baghdad was burning because we were powerless. That night, I discovered another form of guilt and it became the fuel for anger. I should have been bombed alongside my family. But I wasn't.

I'd spent eight years as a coward, not saying a single word for Iraq or making the smallest gesture for it. Now I couldn't disown it any longer. I couldn't ignore it. I ached to think I'd blotted it all out: the country, my family, the sanctions. After the twelve-year blockade that had throttled

Iraq, I'd tossed the UN and international law into the trash. And now that Baghdad was about to fall, I was going to close the lid on it. I'd spent the last eight years in ignorance and naivety. And that night I decided to re-engage with all those interrogative pronouns.

In the sky that had relieved daylight of its duties, I saw the first stars of the world after, and what I really wanted to see again was Iraq and my father and his secret.

FREEDOM

(January 25, 1972)

MY FATHER has never forgotten that day. A Tuesday when Baghdad was in the grips of winter.

Rami was walking through a still-brisk, pinkish mist. A few minutes before the first glimmers of daylight, he paused at Hahi Ali's little stall to buy some sweet cardamom tea and a cheese sandwich in a diamond-shaped bun drizzled with honey. He stopped outside his old apartment building, but neither Hatem nor any of his old friends was waiting for him in his apartment. Were they free? Rami had no idea. They hadn't left a message. He turned with a heavy heart and noticed the janitor sweeping outside his small lodge, but when Rami approached, the man frowned, obviously uncomfortable to see this ghost from the past. He didn't want any trouble with the secret police. Rami was a former prisoner; he couldn't stay there. No, there was no need to pay the outstanding rent. Yes, he could fetch his belongings. The important thing was he needed to leave now and never come anywhere near the building again. The janitor went into his lodge and reappeared with two cases: a Samsonite briefcase and another bag barely any larger. Rami took them and walked away without looking back and without opening the cases.

On that day, at the age of twenty-nine, Rami was about to leave Baghdad. The city's central station was already full of bustle and the mauve glow of dawn was reflected on the asphalt in the square outside. People were saying painful goodbyes—sons kissing their mothers one last time and smelling the crook of their necks, in the hope of remembering this childhood smell for all time. Rami, though, was alone to say his final farewell.

At the same time and in the same city square, quantities of prisoners were released, all wearing the same striped blue shirt given to them by the city's most famous prison—the last palace. Seeing crowds of passengers getting on and off rickety old buses inherited from the British, Rami gathered his wits again. He still had time for a quick smoke. He was nervous and had lost a lot of weight. Since his release he'd been chain-smoking Miami Blues as if, just for the space of a single breath, the smoke could turn his guilty thoughts into a cloud of ash.

My last year before I turn thirty, he thought.

Rami had never left Iraq before, even for a few days. But now, on this day, he was determined to turn the page, to flee the madness that had taken hold of his country, to leave those close to him and take refuge among strangers. All at once he was assailed by a wave of mixed emotions but was actually reassured by his apprehensions: If he was afraid, that meant he was capable of emotion again and so he must be alive. He'd been robbed of everything in prison, his humanity and his innocence. He now seemed to be coming back to life.

The huge square dotted with bus stops was starting to thrum with activity. On that winter morning Rami was convinced that his life would be brighter in France, but he found it hard to take the first step, as if the very land of his country were holding him back. All around him, tears rolled down cheeks. The silent veil of dawn was torn by mothers' cries while apathetic bus drivers slung battered suitcases into the open bellies of their buses.

Rami thought about Muhja. She would definitely have been one of those loving mothers. She would have said her last goodbye to him by asking him never to forget her, to make sure he called home from time to time, to go ahead and live, and to smile at his new life. The mothers' tears afforded him some solace. After all, they were shedding universal tears for all sons. Rami could measure in their eyes the extent of what had been taken from him. He started searching their faces for one that looked like Muhja's, like the hazy impression he still had of her. A luminous face with blue eyes. He didn't find it.

As he climbed onto the bus, he was suddenly aware that his knees were quaking with emotion. Devastated by the goodbyes to which he himself had not been entitled, he realized that he was leaving behind that other country, the past, and perhaps forever. The curtain fell on one last painful scene: departure.

Rami chose a window seat. To his right, a young man of about his age but thinner than he was, stared straight ahead; he seemed to have erected a thick wall between himself and the outside world. Rami paid no attention to his fellow passenger and allowed a discreet tear to fall. When the bus eventually set off, a reverential silence settled over the passengers. Then, for no apparent reason, they drove around the central station three times. The first time perhaps to prolong the sadness of those final moments; the second maybe for the beauty of the cityscape; and the last most likely to give people one last chance to decide against leaving.

A deathly silence. Only the bus's already weary engine groaned in time with its slow progress, as if it too didn't really want to leave Baghdad. But Rami had made up his mind, and as difficult as it might feel, he didn't have a choice. He was sure of that now. In leaving, he couldn't possibly be descending into deeper depths than he'd already experienced. Whatever lay ahead, it would surely offer him wider horizons than the skies over Baghdad.

While he tried to put his thoughts in some sort of order, Rami noticed a man running behind the bus. He rubbed his eyes to check he was seeing right. Hatem! Hatem waving his arms and yelling. Stunned, Rami pressed his good ear to the window. It was pointless, he couldn't hear what Hatem was shouting. At every red light, his friend caught up with the bus, and battled along the sidewalk until, gasping, he drew level with Rami. With his forehead against the glass, Rami watched his friend cup his mouth with his hands and shout something that seemed more important than a good-bye. Sadly, Rami couldn't stop the bus. Or didn't want to. He wasn't the only person running away. And he mustn't give up or change his mind. What was Hatem doing there? Where had he been when Rami was in prison? Was he just reminding him of his friendship and loyalty?

All Rami knew was that France, that faraway place, the country that was to be his future, was waiting for him. He rested his temple against the dirty window to watch the city slip by, the city that had assumed a strange sepia color—it was becoming a part of the past. He turned around one last time, but Hatem had vanished. Had he dreamed it?

The only thing Rami knew for sure was that he was raising anchor for the first time in his life.

ROOM 219

(October 4, 2019)

MY FATHER'S memories stopped there. He couldn't remember what happened after January 25, 1972. Not a single trace of what came next or of his exile. Remembering
anything more was pointless. He now refused newspapers,
couldn't tolerate television, brushed aside his meal trays,
cursed the night staff, and—more than anything else—
loathed mirrors. He couldn't bear the sight of them anymore. He couldn't bear the sight of *him* anymore. However
often I explained that this "other guy" was his reflection,
that he was seventy-five and had a family, a son, a daughter,
a wife, that he liked black coffee with three sugars, that he
enjoyed reading, discussions, and the TV news, he would
shrug with a "What do I know?"

This "other guy," the person he'd once been, was someone he no longer recognized.

The doctor came into the room. Now that he was standing, he seemed less of a savior, more human. He examined

my father for a few minutes—his heartbeat, breathing, and weight.

"Fifty-nine kilos. You must try to eat a bit more, Mr. Ahmed."

I fought back tears. In his prime, my father had weighed ninety kilos. I had no memories of him as a puny figure; he'd always been a well-built man who could tear a telephone directory in half with his bare hands. What had happened to the guy who picked a fight on the subway? When did he get so old? When did he throw in the towel? Did people change bodies overnight? I'd already lost the father I knew before, how could anyone die twice?

He was now just a shadow of his former self. And I resented him for looking so thin. I wanted to ask him to get up and walk, to fight, stop going downhill, eat even if he wasn't hungry, take the subway and buy his newspaper and rebel. I did what all children do at some point in their lives: I switched roles.

"You need to eat, Dad. You need to get your strength back."

"I just can't do it." He showed me his throat. "There's a blockage here."

"I know, but you have to try. We want you back home in good shape."

"I don't remember where home is."

He raised his arms helplessly. He'd even forgotten his own home. All he knew was that his first illness had spawned another. He understood the words *amnesia* and *memory*, and he accepted that I was his son.

I felt an urgent need to talk to him, to reveal what I didn't want him to know, to be the opposite of the secretive father he'd been to me, to tell him that I too had met Hatem.

THE POINT OF NO RETURN

(June 2009)

THE FIRST time I went to Iraq with my father I was the age Rami had been when he'd fled the country.

It was another Iraq. The unthinkable had happened: Baghdad had fallen, and Saddam Hussein had been tried, then executed. Not a single trace of him remained. Incredible that an almost thirty-year reign could be reduced to oblivion like that.

The Americans were the country's new masters. They lived barricaded in what is still called the green zone, a rigorously protected enclave in central Baghdad. The rest of the population, the Iraqis themselves, survived in the red zone.

Ravaged by war, Iraq was broken, gradually dying after six years of American occupation. I'd visited several times in the hope of describing the country, not to my friends anymore but to anyone prepared to read about it. Writing a book on the subject had become an obsession. I suggested several times that my father come with me; together we could find his lost country, thirty-seven years after he'd left. He could help me identify historical markers and meet people, and he meanwhile could reconnect with his past. I'd been nagging him for a while, and he always responded with a circumspect grimace—neither a proper refusal nor true acceptance.

Did he even want to go?

One spring evening, I sensed a fissure in this facade of doubt, and I jumped on the opportunity to ask the question again.

"Why not?" he replied.

———

The journey felt a good deal longer than it had when I was a child. With Iraq no longer respectable in the eyes of the international community, there were no direct flights between Paris and Baghdad. We not only had to make a stopover in Jordan but also needed to board a flight piloted by a South African mercenary. Some planes had been targeted even after the end of the war so a number of airlines had recruited South African pilots who had experience in survival techniques, such as a spin.

During the flight, my father, who was missing his nicotine, seemed anxious. I sat by the window to watch the geometric outline of the Kurdish mountains and eventually the endless flat desert all the way to the shapeless beige smudge of Baghdad. All the passengers were putting on a show of serenity despite the tension in their bodies and faces. Away in the distance, Baghdad looked as immobilized as my thoughts. When we were close enough to land my hands felt clammy, and I put them on my knees to pretend I felt nothing. Everyone stared up at the ceiling or, beyond it, at God. The plane began its descent by circling like a vulture over the remains of Baghdad. Then it dropped in a spin, and we dove through the clouds headfirst. Out the window I saw rectangular forms growing before my eyes until they assumed the shape of humble, sand-colored houses. The airport came into view, a white square among the palm groves. It looked lifeless. Iraq must have been the only place in the world where a pilot had to descend vertically over the airport to avoid possible rocket attacks. My father started to look worried. Would he recognize his country?

The plane landed into a scene from a Hollywood war film. No one clapped. When the door opened, scorching hot air blasted our faces. We were surrounded by armored vehicles, American soldiers, and helicopters hovering overhead. *Apocalypse Now*. The sound of Baghdad was as I'd imagined the occupation: powerlessness in the face of the machinery of war, and a sense of no longer belonging. My father looked completely thrown; he hadn't pictured his country defiled like this and so impoverished.

We held our breath as we traveled along "Route Irish," the death road between the world of the occupiers and that of the occupied. I didn't recognize anything. Charred walls, shell craters, and the black skeletons of what must have been Iraqi military vehicles. All around us, the desert showed traces of the war with glints of ash in its orangy sands. Burned-out cars dotted the roadside, reminders of shocking incidents about which we'd heard reports. And date palms decapitated by an American army impatiently opening up unrestricted sightlines. Those huge headless trees were an omen of the grim future that lay ahead for Iraqis. Dark thoughts escorted us along that lethal stretch of road.

Baghdad's whole face had changed. Never before had I seen so many military vehicles, soldiers, and police officers there. Some of the armed men looked like vigilantes. The taxi driver sounded his horn to plow a route through— horns had always been a whole separate language.

"A short beep means hello," he explained, "two beeps asks a question, and three warns of danger."

The traffic lights had stopped working long ago. Did my father remember the narrow streets of his childhood? My heart sank: Was it a mistake to bring him here? Perhaps it would have been sensible to have left him to his exile. But he decided to stop in the Karrada neighborhood in central Baghdad. And he wanted to be alone.

"I need to find my way around the city, Euphrates. Just for a while, at first, do you understand?" he'd said on the plane.

Yes, I understood. I myself had other plans: I was meeting Saad. Fallujah had become a hideout for armed groups, and I wouldn't be able to go back there yet, so I wanted to hear my uncle talk about my Normandy. My father didn't want to see Saad. They hadn't talked since he'd fled. I was in the middle, a go-between for the stepbrothers, relaying messages for them, and they'd both accepted that.

I left my father at the foot of the Abbas Ibn Firnas statue where a line of taxis waited for passengers. I climbed into an old Peugeot 504. How old was the driver? Seventy, eighty? We crawled along a packed street: Endless checkpoints and the faulty traffic lights had turned the roads into lawless hot spots. Some cars drove the wrong way along the fast lane, others rode up onto the sidewalk to skirt traffic. My driver dodged all the potholes, which he seemed to know by heart.

Like most of his fellow ad hoc taxi drivers, he had three diplomas to his name, but they'd been of little use to him during his lowly career in the old regime's army. The two Gulf Wars in which he'd fought, the sanctions, and lastly the American invasion had put an end to his ambitions as a poet. Like everyone else, he'd been robbed of his dreams. He'd now been doing this for ten years, plying the streets of Baghdad at the wheel of his rusted old car that still held together by some miracle. That was the legacy of twelve years of sanctions: having to do everything with nothing. Twelve years written in people's very skin. And his told a tale of resourcefulness and cunning.

With his cigarette in his mouth and against a background of pop songs that he sang to himself as he eyed me furtively in the rearview mirror, he seemed to want to talk. Every little exchange was cause for an anecdote. When I told him I was fascinated by the ambiance in Iraq's cafés, he took that as an invitation to explain their importance in the country's history. They'd played a key role in the collective subconscious of Iraq. Baghdad's cafés had witnessed events that had had repercussions across the whole country. They were a place for debates and literary discussions but also—during the most difficult times—for political confrontations. In peacetime, they had evenings of music and poetry, and were full of music enthusiasts and lovers of literature like him. But that was in a different age. Now they were places to sing of hardship, talk about war, and dance with the dead. He hadn't set foot in a café since 2003.

"A den of iniquity..."

He seemed nostalgic, lost in faraway thoughts, then he stopped talking abruptly and turned up the radio. It was playing a Baghdadi tune, an Iraqi *maqam*, the same as my father listened to on his Walkman, isolated in the middle of his family, with a bottle of wine by his side.

"Don't stay too long in one place," my driver warned as we emerged from the tunnel toward Tahrir Square. "I can see you're not from here. There are lots of crooks around."

He stubbed out his cigarette on the fascia of his door and dropped me at the traffic circle in Liberation Square. I'd been warned: You should never spend more than fifteen minutes in one place in post-liberation Iraq. People were kidnapped for five hundred dollars. Killing came as easily as drinking a cup of tea.

I had to keep moving so I decided to take my thoughts for a walk. I went along Al Rashid Street and after only a few minutes came across an unexpected sight: ochre-colored pillars and ancient walls damaged by the passage of time and by protests, houses so old they were barely still standing, and their traditional windows—their *moucharabieh*—were like Baghdad's sad eyes.

Al Rashid Street was a bygone world, a world apart. It was here that the Egyptian diva Oum Kalthoum had performed, here that Baghdad's first movie theater had opened its doors, here that modern Iraq's political life had been debated, and here—in its famous cafés—that intellectuals, journalists, and artists had met. It was from here that major demonstrations against the British occupation had set out, here too that, in 1959, Saddam Hussein had made a failed coup against President Abd al-Karim Qasim when his motorcade passed. I had no idea that here, in this same street, my father had campaigned and sung revolutionary hymns.

This street was the heart of historic Baghdad, which—as an homage to Euclid's teachings—had once been a circular city with a two-kilometer diameter. It was named after the caliph Harun al-Rashid from an era when Baghdad was the most remarkable city on the planet. At the time it had set an example as a refined civilization, an image still borne out today by *One Thousand and One Nights*. I now felt it was *that* country that I knew better, my father's country and mine. I took the time to study the city I'd once known and whose images were still engraved on my memory. I wanted to give my imagination free rein in order to feel closer to Rami when he'd been the age I was now. Like a blind man, I used my hands to feel my way through my memories. I walked past prestigious mosques and a number of souks to reach Mutanabbi Street and its big secondhand-book market where collectors strolled for hours in search of a rare find. The humid air smelled of sandy heating oil, the forced marriage between the desert and the hot fuel of electric generators.

I slipped into the skin of the caliph who enjoyed listening to his people talk; he would dress as a beggarman and roam his city's streets. I walked and listened and watched, as young Rami had most likely done. I didn't want to miss anything of the show going on around me. I made my way slowly along the pillars of the long arcade of shops, listening for conversations inside. These snatches of dialogue, and occasional plaintive monologues, came together to form a poem as chaotic as the streets of Baghdad. Scrap-metal merchants with rusty tools alongside antique dealers, jewelers chatting with bakers, booksellers discussing politics with their customers and speculating about rumors in their armchair debates. In all the commotion of the street, I became aware I was being watched.

Sitting on the ground with filthy feet and a face framed by a scarf blackened by exhaust fumes, a child was staring at me. He was selling chewing gum and handkerchiefs but didn't try offering them to me. He looked me up and down, and it felt as if he alone could reveal a truth that I'd fought to find all through my childhood, when I'd been so wide of the mark in trying to imagine little Rami's life: He'd lost his mother, been beaten by Samiya, humiliated by Saad, and stripped bare by life itself.

The child studied my shoes, then looked up at my face. The street children knew everyone who came through here. They got the picture. I felt I'd been unmasked. No more illusions as the caliph in disguise; I was back to being a foreigner. The eye contact may have lasted only a few seconds, but it felt to me like hours. That boy's penetrating gaze allowed me to understand self-evident facts of a scene in which I didn't feature. "The streets of Iraq are strewn with memories of our heroes and our dead. You're not one of them. You're an outsider," the boy's eyes said.

I continued on my way and thought of my father again. Perhaps he had been that child. He had the same look in his eye, a look that spoke of an imploding world. Bottomless eyes, wells of injustice. Eyes that cut through your soul and that you could never forget. And they described my father's childhood without my realizing it. A child with dirty feet who might be an orphan, who might flee his country someday to escape a life lost among the ashes, to build a stable future and dry the blood of the innocent souls he'd left behind.

"Euphrates!"

I jumped in surprise. Saad was standing behind me and the child had disappeared—had he ever existed? As I entertained this thought, Saad took my arm and led me toward Mutanabbi Street, where we sat down in its legendary café, the Shabandar. Saad had things to tell me.

He and his brothers had been fired immediately after the invasion. One of the first steps the Americans had taken was to purge any institution with close or even distant links to Saddam Hussein. Military personnel, party executives, scientists, teachers...a million civil servants had lost their jobs. Iraq had gone from an ultra-authoritarian regime to security desert overnight. The state had become an empty shell that needed filling quickly and the net result was long lines of Iraqis coming to volunteer at police precincts every day. Bakers, mechanics, taxi drivers...anyone could become a police officer and carry a gun. The unemployed were reticent at first but they faced a stark choice: try to survive the recession with unreliable casual work or join a branch of the insurrection.

And then Saad finally gave me news of Fallujah. The Americans had seen it as a pariah ever since two all-terrain vehicles had been ambushed there. Four men, three of them American, had been executed by a group of insurgents, and their corpses mauled by an angry crowd. The mutilated bodies of the victims, who'd been security envoys for the Bush administration, were hung from the green bridge. For the Americans, the real war had started in Fallujah, where they had to tackle an invisible enemy lying in ambush. It then continued in Baghdad and across the rest of the country.

"Fallujah was proclaimed as the seat of resistance, and America decided to wipe us out. Fallujah's going to be destroyed."

My father's hometown was on the front page of all the papers. We weren't allowed to go there. Everything smelled of death and the soccer stadium was now a cemetery.

Saad also told me there were rumors of war and said I needed to listen to them.

"If you want to get out alive, you need to pay attention to them."

Helicopter blades slicing through the milky sky, ambulance sirens, and shots fired—they were all indicators. They set the tempo for each day in a macabre dance that was becoming instinctive. A car bomb exploding nearby reverberated all the way inside your guts. Shells gave off a strong, clear sound. Improvised mines hurled hot air into your face and sand into your mouth.

"In Baghdad we stand on our doorsteps, listening to this deadly music," Saad told me. "Iraqis have only two options: Go out and risk dying, or stay shut away inside and don't live at all."

The capital was emptying of its inhabitants. The few remaining residents were holed up inside their homes, and inside themselves.

Saad and I parted not knowing whether we would ever see each other again. I had to get back to my father and avoid lingering in the streets.

The Fallujah Café wasn't far away, the taxi driver had assured me. It stood at the top of Sadoun Street, one of the capital's major thoroughfares whose surface reflected the sun's glare so powerfully it was blinding. I kept going until I could just about make out the café's sign. The café looked out over the Tigris, which bounced the light back just as brightly, so the café's name wasn't legible until you were ensconced in the little pocket of shade between the street and the river. If you stood with your back to the place, you could see half of Baghdad spread out at your feet.

Seen from above, Baghdad looked like any other city, a far cry from the violence of those last six years. But from close up, the war was visible on every street corner, in people's faces and on their bodies. Black figures everywhere— women to whom no one paid any attention but who were the living ghosts of a country haunted by war. Black widows.

I met my father at the Fallujah Café with only one thought in my mind: From now on nothing would be *too complicated* and I wasn't *too young* anymore. This wasn't Stop Cluny. The time had come. As its name implied, the café had become a sanctuary for inhabitants of Fallujah. The huge space, full of nargileh smokers and tea sippers, was crammed with tables and chairs, reverberating to bursts of raised voices and the slap of dominoes and backgammon counters on glass tables. I spotted my father at the very back, deep in conversation with a man who was waving his arms around. When I reached them, they both stood up.

"I'd like to introduce Hatem, my childhood friend. We haven't seen each other for more than thirty years, can you believe it?"

"Are you Rami's son? You're so tall! Did you know you have me to thank for being called Euphrates? Did your father tell you the story?"

"What?" I asked, looking at my father.

"Later, mine son, I'll tell you later."

"You know, the last time I talked to your father was here in this café. It was called the Mahdawi then, and it was where politicos met. Now it's a place for nostalgia freaks like us two, people trying to run away from old age. We always get drawn back to our roots, whether we like it or not."

"And this was where I stood up for you against those Baath Party thugs," my father added.

"It's the same old story," Hatem went on, smiling at me. "The person who teaches you to swim is the one who ends up drowning. Here, come on, let's talk. I think we should go out onto the terrace, we can't hear a thing in here!"

Hatem. I'd never heard of him until then. Rami hadn't told me anything about his childhood friend—nor any other friends, for that matter. He and my father seemed very close, as if the decades of separation were just minutes.

The three of us sat at a small round table that reminded me of those at Stop Cluny. Hatem was fingering prayer beads. He talked, mimicked, described, and my father laughed. I'd rarely seen him like this. There was a taste of childhood to the Fallujah Café, and Hatem's stories were exhilarating. From time to time, a waiter would bring us fresh cups of tea without asking any questions—Iraqi tea had its own rituals. Once you have a cup of it in front of you, friendships can be forged, or undone.

The past resurfaced as they talked. I listened as they remembered summers spent diving into the Euphrates, how strict Mr. Fadil had been, their university days, the

Karrada neighborhood, their forbidden loves, the fates of various acquaintances, the deaths of others—escape for those who'd been able to, and death for those who hadn't. I looked from one to the other, studying them, their gestures, their former lives, and the way they drank their tea. I desperately wanted to talk to them, but the opportunity didn't arise.

In my pocket my hand hovered over the small card that I'd taken from my father's briefcase. The one that bore a name I didn't recognize. I was waiting for the right moment to ask the question that had been plaguing me since my childhood. But the spoons were still stirring, and the sugar was still slowly dissolving in their cups. And I just went on listening to them and laughing. Right up until fate decided otherwise.

I noticed two teenagers watching us from a couple of tables to my right. One of them took a piece of paper from his pocket and the other nodded imperceptibly. Then they sprang to their feet and one of them came over to our table and took a gun from inside his shirt. I just had time to see the barrel wrapped in sticky tape—a homemade silencer. The young man pointed the gun toward us perfectly calmly and fired. Three rounds. At regular intervals. A sample of the noises of war that Saad hadn't described to me.

Pok-pok-pok.

The panicking crowd surged inside the café, carrying us with it. It all happened in the space of a few seconds. Through the window the facts were clear: Just one person was still sitting at a table in the middle of the now empty terrace, his head slightly tilted. Hatem hadn't moved. Blood trickled down his forehead. His shirt was bright with light reflected by the glass tables. The color of his face had already changed. I'll never forget what my father said then: "But why didn't he follow us inside?"

He didn't seem to understand.

"Dad, Hatem's just been assassinated. He was the target."

Several police officers stationed some twenty meters away hadn't moved. They casually smoked their cigarettes as the crowd dispersed. The shooters had fired quite openly. I can still remember their childlike but determined faces, their confident body language, their icy eyes, and their self-possession. It wasn't the first time they'd killed.

For a long moment, my father and I just stood there near the bar, waiting for who knew what. The smell of nargileh had been replaced by the smell of death and gunpowder. My father was as pale as his shirt. As we'd fled inside, I'd instinctively gripped his collar to haul him in with all my strength. I looked at his watch. It was broken. It read: 17:54.

When the ambulance arrived, Hatem was put onto a stretcher. I thought back to the drug addict who'd overdosed near my home when I was seven. I didn't have the courage to approach Hatem's body, not wanting to see those blue blotches again. Everyone else was keeping their distance anyway. And my father didn't move either, he'd turned to stone. We stood in silence until the ambulance had left. My father had no address for Hatem and no names for anyone close to him. Did he have children? A wife? It had all happened so quickly. Out of nowhere the skies opened with driving rain. I had a strange feeling that the deluge was washing away the excretions of the world, cleansing the asphalt of the black filth of humanity and the unspeakable act that had just taken place. In Iraq, rain is synonymous with blessing, and some people raised their hands heavenward. Then, as if surfacing from a dream, the café owner announced he was shutting up and he cursed this life. Yes, we could shelter there till the rain stopped. We left the café a few minutes later, but Rami would never shake off that storm.

Death had crash-landed at 17:54, and for the rest of Rami's life that would be the tipping point between before and after, the new "now" that would last for years. Without a word, without any extraneous movement, he followed me to the taxi I'd just hailed. More than thirty years' absence. A few minutes of reunion. I could see the death of a whole world in my father's eyes. And that death had struck at 17:54. Rami was silently bowing under the weight of loss. But we were free. Free and alive.

My sleep was disturbed by bad dreams. Hatem's murder, the panic, my father's ashen face. Those two teenagers fired at us all night. At dawn I heard women wailing outside.

"Yaboooooo! Yaboooooooooooooooooo!"

Lamentations. A group of women had come to howl other people's pain and the loss of a soul. It was a way of defying misfortune and vocalizing the injustices enshrined in law. I opened the small transom that overlooked the street from where I could hear the voices. It was an *asifa* day, with a storm of red sand slowly engulfing the neighborhood. The women's wailing continued regardless; nothing could stop this proclamation of death. I shuddered. And then I saw them, they were clustered around a coffin strapped to the roof of a car. A funeral procession that had become commonplace to those still alive. I thought about Hatem. And my father. Why was I crying? I hadn't known Hatem. I'd only seen him for about ten minutes. I clung to the edge of the washbasin. Those women, that sandstorm, the deaths...I was crying for my Iraq, the one I'd come looking for, the one my father had hoped to see again. I looked through the little window one last time—the voices and the shadows were fading, swallowed by the storm, smothered by it. A rare moment of respite in the Baghdad that I was inflicting on my father.

Rumors came even more quickly than burials: It was already being whispered that Hatem collaborated with the Americans, he met them in the green zone and had been seen stepping out of a military vehicle. It was claimed that he signed contracts with war mercenaries who were there to rebuild the country, using oil money that was supposed to come to the Iraqi people. There were also rumors that Hatem had already survived an assassination attempt, that the sniper had only just missed him but had hit his translator, and that his death was inevitable, he was a traitor and collaborators' names were circulated on lists handed out by armed gangs outside mosques and in cafés and on the Internet.

My father said he didn't want to stay any longer, he wanted to leave this wretched country for good. He didn't open his mouth once on our way to the airport the following day. Rami was turning his back on his country for a second time.

Once home, he did what he'd been postponing for all those years: He applied for French nationality.

ROOM 219

(October 5, 2019)

STILL REELING from my description of what happened at the Fallujah Café, my father was slowly regaining his composure when he gave a sudden wail. I went over to him and put a hand on his shoulder. He was crying. He seemed to be reliving the scene. The one in the café? Hatem's death? I begged him to confide in me and tell me what was going on inside his head. He sobbed, pressed his shaking hands to his ears, closed his eyes, and shook his head. We stayed there facing each other, unmoving. I was worried—why had I told him about that trip to Baghdad and our meeting with Hatem?

Time stood still in room 219. I looked at my father and couldn't help thinking about the swirling chaos. Everything is born and lives and dies in a maelstrom, a whirlpool—just like the one that nearly drowned my father.

Before he lost his memory, all he had was cancer, which was enough in itself. It was there the whole time, in his every breath, his every move, in the electrocardiogram that acted as a clock, and in the seconds that ticked by to the rhythm of his heartbeat. Between his chemotherapy sessions, life swung like a pendulum from waiting to anxiety. Until now, amnesia—that interloper in our confidences—had become something of an ally. It hovered over us and pointed its finger at us and dribbled onto my guilt and his merciful ignorance. But this invisible enemy encouraged us to express things we'd never managed to tell each other—and by "we," I mean the we that kept us shut away in room 219.

Just for a moment, the amnesia disappeared. In my research I'd learned that this was called a lifting of amnesia and that it often happened at times of intense emotion. Childbirth, an accident, a key conversation reawakening buried trauma.

"I remember."

I saw a different father, and sat down next to him. I'd waited my whole life for this moment: talking rather than watching him die, using every means at our disposal. For a long time, I'd avoided the possibility of really talking to him, of making this precious exchange a living thing. I'd been looking for this missing story my whole life.

"Amir Mullah," I said quietly.

He looked at me.

"The card. Does Amir Mullah mean anything to you?" I persisted.

He nodded. He remembered.

It was a little while before he could speak again. I thought of Stop Cluny and my night in custody at the police precinct, the missed opportunities for a proper conversation. Our attenuating circumstance was finally about to happen. The whirlpool of years had stayed faithful to him. Exile never erases the past.

He took a long drag on his cigarette, then stubbed it out and looked at me. The memory seemed to weigh as heavily on him as those watermelons he once buried in the depths of the river.

"I'm listening, Dad."

"What do you want to know?"

I detected something I'd heard before—his voice from Stop Cluny, a dwindling voice and a disappearing body. What I wanted to know?

Did he remember the Fallujah Café? And Hatem's death? And the card with the false name? I edged closer to him, and he looked up at me again.

Nurses laughing in the corridor. The rhythmic rattle of a trolley distributing insipid meals. I closed the door, I wanted to get this done. I was ready. The version of my father who'd been hidden in that briefcase needed to be set free; it was now or never.

"I was Amir Mullah. It was my activist name."

Rami and Amir were two sides of the same coin, he told me. Everything he'd told me about the Mahdawi Café in the 1960s was true. It wasn't Rami who went there, but Amir Mullah, a Trotskyist activist who opposed Qasim's regime. He was one of the infamous "last customers" at the back of the room. And Amir Mullah didn't go home alone. Neither had he parted company with Hatem that evening.

AMIR MULLAH

(Summer 1963)

THE STORY dated back to July 1963; my father was sure of that.

On July 14 every year, the Mahdawi Café celebrated the 1958 revolution, and the Iraqi government insisted on having official photographs of each anniversary. Members of land, sea, and air forces, civil servants in the country's ministries—everyone had to comply. It was also a way of taking a census, and reminding people that they were being watched.

Rami went to the café, ready for the occasion.

"Three cheers for the revolution!" the photographer said automatically.

Yes, three cheers for the coup, thought Rami.

The photographer was absorbed in his work, clearly a perfectionist.

"Look away into the distance... I mean, as if you were looking at the sea."

"Okay. Like this?" Rami asked, slightly tilting up his chin, amused by the photographer's commitment to a revolution that the man most likely believed was real.

"Yes, don't move. That's perfect!"

Poor man. Rami sighed. How can he believe in this charade?

And what was this all for? It was in the name of a revolution that had changed nothing. People were still hungry, and violence reigned supreme. To Rami, the revolution had been a coup in disguise, and one coup inevitably leads to another. Followed by plenty more.

The country had changed. This year, 1963, didn't bode well, Rami thought. The government was nationalizing its oil, educating its people, modernizing its infrastructure, calling for Arab unity, all in the guise of progress, but it had declared war on its opponents and was hiding a profusion of violence in the shadowy corridors of its security services. And, in the throes of the Cold War, Iraq was being eyed covetously by two major powers pitted against each other: the United States and the Soviet Union.

"Come on! Imagine you're looking at the sky," the photographer now suggested earnestly.

"Oh, I can look at the sky every day but it's the birds who watch me," Rami said jokingly.

The photographer didn't react. He was too busy: A long line of men in uniform was waiting behind him.

Rami had agreed to meet Hatem at the Mahdawi that evening. His friend was a fervent critic of the "false revolution"; he was smoldering inside and wanted to continue the fight. Rami spotted him at the back of the café, where they held their secret meetings away from the prying eyes of Baath supporters. Hatem was sipping his tea with a strange compulsion, and Rami knew him well enough to know that their conversation would be serious.

"Are you free this evening?" was Hatem's opening gambit.

"Hatem…"

"We have an important meeting at ten o'clock, you need to come. Things are underway, Rami. Your name's come up several times among the comrades and people want to know if you're with us, if we can count on you. Or not."

"I've told you what I think, Hatem. I'm neither for it nor against it. But tell me honestly, what do you think it will change?"

Hatem stared at him intently for a while. Rami felt as if his friend was reading his mind, trying to find the fault line.

"You do see what this regime's doing, don't you?" Hatem said. "We've been asked to bomb villages, but do you remember where the two of us are from? Are you sure there were just soldiers in those houses? And what about the activists who are arrested every day and tortured? Should we just forget about them? Should we let them die?"

"Oh, because you think the methods will change? If we overturn the regime, then what happens? It'll just get worse, Hatem. Do you want to replace one single-party system with another?"

"I hope you're right, my friend. Either way, we're crossing the bridge. We're going to ambush them. And we'll drive them out of the country with or without you."

———————

That same evening, Qasim left the Ministry of Defense and headed home to his huge villa guarded by tanks and dozens of soldiers. As usual, he climbed into his Land Rover and sat on the right-hand side of the rear seat. The driver and an aide-de-camp in the front of the vehicle were his only escort. The car set off down Al Rashid Street, which was the city's main thoroughfare despite how narrow it was. It was about six o'clock. The presidential car, which was instantly recognizable, made slow progress because of the rush-hour traffic. On the sidewalks, a milling crowd of pedestrians, beggars, shoeshine men, and shopkeepers started clapping. No one noticed the ten men standing motionless behind the pillars along the street.

When the car turned into Sadoun Street, each of the ten men took a machine gun from his loose dishdasha and opened fire on General Qasim. With lightning reflexes, the general drew his revolver and managed to shoot one of his assailants before he in turn was hit and collapsed. The crowd dispersed rapidly, and traders closed up their little stores with sheet metal. This brief moment of confusion allowed the attackers to escape through the souk along a narrow street.

When the police arrived in the now deserted street, Qasim was lying on the rear seat, badly wounded but alive. Unfortunately, his driver had not been so lucky. The general was taken to the hospital and came away with fractures in his left shoulder and arm. The man who hit him could not be identified, which stoked the mood of mistrust and paranoia. Martial law and strict curfews were introduced the very next day.

The emotional response of the people and the popularity of a man who'd miraculously survived an assassination attempt were perfect circumstances in which to intensify the fight against opponents and other conspiracy theorists. The general gave orders for several officers to be executed, and a press conference was held in the hospital where he was still convalescing.

"A number of officers and traitors have been executed," he announced. "They were renegades. They had been turned into heroes in this revolution that means so much to us, but they are heroes only in betrayal. Their executions are a warning to anyone who may be tempted to betray their country."

Rami's apartment was searched from top to bottom at dawn. But Rami no longer existed, he was now called Amir. Amir Mullah.

THE LAST DAY

(October 5, 2019)

I DIDN'T recognize my father, even though my mother had warned me. Chemotherapy was destroying him physically. He was wasting away and had lost his hair and eyebrows. I'd been away for just a few days, and the cancer had reclaimed him. I'd been calling for news and my mother and sister had taken turns by his bedside in my absence. In the last few weeks, we'd decided to ease up on the family protocol: My father needed to get used to his wife and daughter again, his family. He needed to see them.

He seemed to be no longer coping with the chemotherapy. When he wasn't sleeping, he said dark, disturbing things.

"It's all over, mine son," he announced when he saw me.

With glaring hypocrisy, I told him this was just a nasty blip, a difficult phase, and everything would get back to normal. I wished he'd refused to be seen in this state, hadn't deigned to listen to my lies, had asked me to leave and said he'd rather be forgotten while he recovered. But no, he wanted me there, he needed my help to go to the bathroom, straighten his pillow, and open the window. My father was frightened. I'd never known him to show fear before. And I was ashamed to feel irritated by it, ashamed that I couldn't understand the man he now was. I stayed with him till the evening, then kissed his forehead and went home. And once again I fell asleep full of anxiety.

That night I had a dream.

It was cold. I was on the roof of a tower so tall I couldn't see anything of the world below. There was a strong, gusting wind. In my right hand I held a cluster of brightly colored balloons. A gentle but insistent breath of wind carried me into the air. Up I sailed, not panicking, and I hung over the city for a while, feeling light and calm. Another man holding balloons flew a few meters over my head, then sank gracefully down to my level. We looked at each other for a while, hanging there in the sky. In his eyes I could see stories of bullying and beatings, of life's humiliations and suffering, of weariness and boredom, and of his need to sweep it all aside, to leave and forget.

The man introduced himself.

I am absence.

I could no longer make out his face, which was suddenly ringed with light. I closed my eyes to concentrate on what he was saying. He quoted a few lines.

The intoxication of this world is mortal, and you and I, my dear friends, are caught up in a winged dream, in the whirlpool of forgetfulness. I am absence.

I couldn't find anything to say in reply. What could I say except that I wanted to succeed where he felt he'd failed?

Then we were on the ground, still holding our balloons, beside a slow steady river. We stood side by side, looking across to the far bank. I felt an irresistible need to go home, and to wake up. I turned to look at my father.

Are you coming, shall we go home?

He didn't say anything for a while, then pointed to a silhouette on the far bank.

I can't, mine son, Muhja's waving to me. Can you see her? She's asking me to go home.

The luminous face gradually transformed into the one I'd always known. My father's hesitant smile was the same as it had always been.

Then everything became a tangle. The balloons popped...

A dizzying fall.

A feeling of dying.

And I woke gasping, paralyzed by what I'd just seen.

A bad dream, a nightmare, a truth. I desperately wanted to call my father, to hear his voice, to ask him questions, and to hear him reply: *It's too complicated.*

He didn't pick up. He would never pick up again. I would never hear his voice again.

GOODBYE, DAD

(October 6, 2019)

IT HAPPENED at dawn. On the other end of the line my mother was in tears: "He's gone." Incredulity at first. Then the injustice of it. And lastly nausea. I hung up. I couldn't find the words, or the strength. I wasn't there.

I headed over by scooter, jumping a red light, taking avenue d'Iéna, then cutting through via rue Georges Bizet. I was talking out loud without even realizing it, endlessly whispering into the wind, *My father, my father, my father.* He had to exist. Still. Whatever the price.

I was on my way over to bring him the missing piece of his story, to complete the circle, because I hadn't told him everything. And I didn't know how to reveal it to him.

What happened next is hazy in my mind. I couldn't see anything or hear anything. It all happened so quickly. Far too quickly, I was guided through the rituals and torn away from my thoughts. The body being washed, being taken to a cold room, the mosque, the funeral prayer, for a man who said he wasn't a believer but referenced God with every promise and used plenty of *Insha'Allah* to suit the person with whom he was talking.

Then a white shroud tucked in a wooden coffin. My father down on the ground.

I wanted to cry out, to give some texture to my pain, but I restrained myself. I stood in silence before that wooden box. How could my father, such a huge personality, a man who had fled Iraq and taken refuge in France, who'd been through the last palace and been tortured, how could he fit in there?

Surrounded by far more strangers than friends or relations, we set off toward the Mont-Valérien cemetery in pelting rain. The raindrops streaming down from my forehead mingled with my tears. My father's coffin was buffeted between the Tigris and the Euphrates, the two rivers adopting each other's curves to form the Shatt al-Arab before launching into a sea of sadness. A deluge for people's eyes, for the eyes of those who'd stopped crying, for the eyes of the absent, an homage from the sky set to the rhythm of spades clinking as constantly and regularly as a clock. The implacable clock of life.

And when my father's coffin was lowered into the ground, I thought of the forecourt of Notre-Dame and Stop Cluny and the conversations we didn't have. I remembered the difficult question he'd suddenly come up with in room 219. Have I made a success of my life? I tried to find the words. The words I would have liked to give him. Dad, you're being buried, and I'm lost in my thoughts.

Dad, you sold postcards on that forecourt for fifteen years. You walked up and down those slippery paving stones, keeping an eye out to avoid being caught by the police. I've done the math. You sold an average of twenty postcard accordions a day, and each accordion had ten cards. In fifteen years, you must have sold more than a hundred thousand cards. Dad, I kiss every one of those cards, I kiss every person who didn't ignore you, who thought about you, who exchanged a smile with you.

Dad, you did us the honor of sacrificing yourself for us, for Arwa, for Mom, and for me. You survived the black wolves, you languished in the last palace, you sacrificed your dreams, you coped with the vacant stares of gawkers as you were reluctantly led away by police officers, you waited in dank cells in police precincts, you took the first and last high-speed subways on Line A and breathed its sulfurous smell every day. My poor father, my hero, you passed on your values to me, and that is my greatest asset. May your sacrifice bear fruit, may Iraq and the Euphrates, the cradle of your life, go on forever.

Dad, you can count on me. I will sing that song on your grave, the one Muhja used to sing. Dad, I crossed the river for you. I crossed the river to drown your wounds. I no longer resent you, my father, now that I've become like you: deaf, mute, and blind in the face of the utter madness that is life.

Go, Rami, go over to the far shore, there are no dangerous whirlpools now, no watermelons to bury, or children to impress, or sorrows to forget, or life to regret, or dreams to curse. Gone are the evils of your magnificent and silent river.

After the interment, I noticed three men a little distance away. They were very elegant in three-piece suits, with hats and pocket squares, standing under umbrellas. I'd never seen them before. They were the same age as my father. They were from far away, from over there perhaps. They came up to the grave and each in turn threw in a handful of dirt. One after the other, they took a few steps back and bowed.

Then they nodded at me and left.

I waited till they'd gone to be alone with you.

Dad, can you hear me inside your little wooden box? Have you taken out your pack of cigarettes? There's this missing story, this story you forgot—but did you really forget it?—thanks to your characteristic reserve. So listen up, because here are the bare facts. The facts I should have told you.

Dad, you weren't thrown into prison by chance. As you may have guessed, you were denounced. Not by a member of Saddam Hussein's police force, nor a political opponent, nor some vengeful person whose pride you hurt, but by your stepmother, Dad. By Samiya.

Yes, Samiya informed on you. You should have died in the last palace, never come out of there, disappeared forever. But do you know who saved you, Dad? It was Saad, Saad whose voice you heard, who was a member of the commando unit that came to arrest you. Did you really forget?

Saad, your stepbrother, your brother in spite of everything, was watching over you. On the way to the last palace, he destroyed all the evidence. Your coup, your leaflets, your weapon. It all disappeared. Saad, who'd set a trap for you as a boy, causing you to lose half your hearing and half your dignity in your father's eyes, decided to save your life in the end. The black scorpions were no longer lethal, and I completely forgot to tell you that.

———————

I now know. Memory is a chosen art, a blank canvas over which we trail paintbrushes, producing results a far cry from exact reality but close to a subjective truth, the truth that inhabits us in the moment that we experience it. Memory isn't necessarily a faithful reproduction of what really happened. It holds on just as readily to both what it wants and what it can't abide.

Photos never tell the whole truth. By freezing time, they immortalize a smile and anchor a memory without surrendering the lies or secrets. We think we know our loved ones but we can't see their gray areas, nor the obscuring veils, nor the whispering, nor what's been forgotten. Sometimes, if we feel like it, photos can allow us to swim through the meanderings of memory, to rewind the clock and re-experience an emotion, but they blinker us in a bygone world.

Memory is a lie that walks just on the right side of truth, and words reveal only one representation of the facts. I didn't let you down, Rami. I described your dream to you, Dad, the one you couldn't reach. And it would have taken me thirty years to achieve. We lied to each other, perhaps as a better way of telling each other the truth, a truth that our own reserve stopped us from expressing. Yes, Dad, you passed on your silence to me. And silence is neither a truth nor a lie.

I can now give you an answer to your question. Yes, you made a success of your life—mine is just a delusion in comparison. Where your dream ran aground, I in turn dreamed. I know who I am, I know where I'm from, thanks to you. I've emptied my invisible suitcase of bad dreams. I've grasped the fact that, instead of letting time hurtle toward oblivion, we must hold on to it, imprint it in our memories, write it and speak it, and perhaps make it the most beautiful thing there is in this life. Living forever through whoever remembers.

ACKNOWLEDGMENTS

FIRST OF all, I would like to thank my mother and my sister who, as well as supporting me, gave me their valuable help throughout the writing process for this book. Memory and imagination are two boundless worlds.

Thank you to my partner, Claire Davanne, for her support, her patience, her willingness to listen, and her shoulder.

Thank you to my dear Catherine Nabokov, a diamond of a literary agent who has become a close friend and who asked me, over a Parisian coffee, if I "didn't feel like writing a novel," a question that triggered this literary adventure.

I must also thank all those who sowed seeds along the way as I wrote, all those who encouraged, listened, advised, read, came on the journey, and offered their support, and I know how lucky I am: Isabelle Pailler, Gregory Messina, Rania Cherfi, Henriette Souk, Eva Baldassari, Marianne

Levy-Leblond, Sidonie Mangin, Thomas Zribi, Bethsabee Zarka, Hugo Van Offel, Saïd Mahrane, Michel Welterlin, Amira Souilem, Nazim Abdelouahab, Dominique Davanne, Sérigne M'Baye Gueye (Disiz), Jean-Pierre Canet, Romain Icard, Tania de Montaigne, Sameer Ahmad, Shathil Nawaf Taqa, Marc Alexandre Oho Bambe, and I'm bound to be forgetting people.

Thank you to my dear editor, Véronique Cardi, for her faith in me and her enthusiasm, and her incredible team: Anne Pidoux for her essential rereading and our long conversations, Charlotte Rousseau, Claire Charles, Vincent Eudeline, and Typhaine Cormier.

Thank you to my family in Iraq for my unique childhood during summers spent in such a distinctive country. A thought for the forgotten and the exiled, and for oppressed dreamers. A thought for you, Dad, who opened the door for me, the door to your lost Iraq.

ABOUT THE AUTHOR

FEURAT ALANI is a French journalist and documentary filmmaker who has spent more than seventeen years reporting across the Middle East. He's the author of two graphic novels, *Le Parfum d'Irak* (Flavors of Iraq), which won the Prix Albert-Londres, France's highest journalism prize, in 2019; and *Falloujah, ma campagne perdue* (Fallujah, my lost campaign). His work has appeared in a variety of international outlets including the *Wall Street Journal, Washington Post, Le Monde Diplomatique,* France 24, *Mediapart,* Al Jazeera, Arte, Canal Plus, and Radio Canada. His debut novel, *I Remember Fallujah,* received the Arab Literature Prize and the Senghor First Novel Prize, and was a finalist for the Goncourt First Novel Prize. He lives in France and Dubai.

ABOUT THE TRANSLATOR

ADRIANA HUNTER studied French and Drama at the University of London. She has translated more than ninety books, including Anka Muhlstein's *Camille Pissarro: The Audacity of Impressionism* and Hervé Le Tellier's *The Anomaly* and *Eléctrico W,* winner of the French-American Foundation's 2013 Translation Prize in Fiction. She lives in Kent, England.